THROUGH THE EYES OF JOHN

THE ANNIHILATION OF NATIONS
A Walk Through Heaven, Earth, and Hell

J.M. Joseph

THROUGH THE EYES OF JOHN:
THE ANNIHILATION OF NATIONS
A Walk Through Heaven, Earth, and Hell
Copyright © 2022 by J.M. Joseph

All rights reserved. No part of this publication may be reproduced, distributed, or transmitted in any form or by any means, including photocopying, recording, or other electronic or mechanical methods, without the prior written permission of the author who is the copyright owner, except in the case of brief quotations embodied in critical reviews and certain other noncommercial uses permitted by copyright law.

ISBN: (Paperback)   978-1-63945-500-3
         (eBook)   978-1-63945-501-0

The view expressed in this book are solely those of the author and do not necessarily reflect the views of the publisher, and the publisher hereby disclaims any responsibility for them.

Writers' Branding
1800-608-6550
www.writersbranding.com
orders@writersbranding.com

CONTENTS

PART I: THE ANNIHILATION OF NATIONS 1
    PHYSICAL AND SPIRITUAL WARFARE 3
    DESTROY THE FAITH OF PEOPLE
    THROUGH THE CHURCH..11
    DESTROY THE MORALS OF PEOPLE,
    THEIR FAMILIES, AND SOCIETY 33
    DESTROY A NATION'S GOVERNMENT............................41
    THE AFTERMATH OF THE SIEGE AND
    INSURRECTION REVEALS THE LACK OF
    CONSTITUTIONAL INSIGHT, CLARITY, AND
    STANDARDS OF ETHICS..53
    AMERICA NEEDS TO BE AWAKEN 63

PART II: PROLOGUE - A WALK-THROUGH
    HEAVEN, EARTH, AND HELL 85
    INTRODUCTION TO JOHN 89
    WHY ARE ANIMALS, PLANTS, AND
    NONLIVING SEEN WITH CONSCIOUSNESS
    IN THE HIERARCHY OF EXISTENCE?................................99
    LET THE SHARING OF EXPERIENCES BEGIN 105
    ON SPIRITUAL CONFRONTATIONS 149

    BIBLIOGRAPHY 163

THROUGH THE EYES OF JOHN

This book shares how nations are presently being destroyed by different sources. As John walked along the path towards spiritual guidance, unknowingly, the turmoil and obstacles that he faced revealed to him later on in life what he was being shown, both in the annihilation of nations and the guidance for souls.

By J.M. Joseph

(RLPJCS)

Dear Reader,

All references for this book are listed immediately after its statements within the writing itself. Therefore, there is no traditional bibliography at the end of this book.

However, a Guidance section from A Steep Climb, by J.M. Joseph, Writers' Branding relaunched in 2021, is included at the end of this book with its respective bibliography.

All references to Sacred Scriptures are from various Christian Bibles.

The author is grateful to all who contributed in any fashion and to those listed in all references and for the permissions extended to be included in this book.

This book is dedicated to the Blessed Trinity, God Our Heavenly Father, His Son Jesus Christ Who has come in the flesh, and the Holy Spirit, Spouse of Mary Immaculate.

O Mary, conceived without sin, pray for us who have recourse to you.

PART I

THE ANNIHILATION OF NATIONS

Introduction

The inception of this book began in the early 70s and its writing in 2011, and now through different lenses in 2017 until the present time. It started in search of spiritual guidance by John, which was related to his spiritual experiences as contained in Part II of this book. Part I is the result of that journey which unexpectedly revealed so much to John. It is not meant to remonstrate or expostulate, but to just share the dichotomy of experiences of one person, what he saw, his viewpoint, and those of others. It is hoped that you, dear reader, will find it interesting and especially helpful, whether you are in agreement, or not at all. The choice is yours and is to be respected.

"And there was war in heaven: Michael and his angels fought against the dragon, and the dragon fought and his angels, and prevailed not; neither was their place found anymore in heaven. And the great dragon was cast out, that old serpent, called the Devil, and Satan, which deceived the whole world: he was **cast out into the earth," (where humans would live),** "and his angels were cast out with him." REVELATION 12:7-9

"How art thou **fallen from heaven,** O Lucifer, son of the morning! How art thou **cut down to the ground which didst weaken the nations!** For the devil said in his heart, 'I will ascend into heaven, I will exalt my throne above the stars of God: I will also sit upon the mount of the congregation, in the sides of the north: I will ascend above the heights of the clouds: I will be like the Highest.'" ISAIAH 14: 12-14

LET THE BATTLES BEGIN, DEAR READER

"We have a wrestling, not against blood and flesh, but against the governments, against the authorities, against the world rulers of this darkness, against the wicked spirit forces in the heavenly places." EPHESIANS 6:12

PHYSICAL AND SPIRITUAL WARFARE

THE ANNIHILATION OF NATIONS
can occur **firstly,** due to many **natural** causes such as large-scale earthquakes, catastrophic tsunamis, endless flooding,

OR

Secondly, it can be launched **without** - through physical warfare, the use of forceful tactics that will kill people, and their lands, such as, with deadly military atomic/nuclear bombings, germs warfare, controlling earth's weather and destruction of environmental factors that can affect the consumption of food, water, medicine, and the air we breathe. It can also involve the use of electromagnetic fields and sources of energy to cause death and destruction, some deliberate, some as a by-product of climate change due to actions of humankind, such as hurling bombs towards the core of the earth, the misuse or overuse of carbon causing elements, the use of ocean and outer space elements pitting nation against nation, and only for one nation's own gain, and the list continues on,

OR

Thirdly, from **within** - the coercive controlling of a nation's belief system through the minds of their citizenry through the infiltration of the spiritual, emotional, and the safety net of individuals from their beliefs, FAITH, or religions of their churches and their leaders. Other areas of attacks are the family structure, manipulating and constant brainwashing the thinking of the adults and children that would lead to negative behaviors towards self or the destruction of others- the society in general, and the nation's economics and businesses through their government, political leaders, laws, and the electoral, judiciary and military systems.

HOW CAN SUCH DESTRUCTION TAKE PLACE FROM WITHIN ON A GRAND SCALE WITH ALL EYES WATCHING?

Infiltration in a manipulative manner is how this occurs.

1. Actions, intentions, or even statements are deliberately made to appear good on a grand scale and as highly worthy causes, but in reality, are done to cover up deceitful and destructive intentions of manipulations which are revealed suddenly or as time goes by. It operates as the serpent in the Garden of Eden.

2. Another way is through fear spearheaded by negative powers such as the redundancy of lies after lies that brainwashes the mind, creating the blindness of ignorance that demolishes truths, resulting in confusion and believing the lies as truths. This then creates a cult or groups of people banning together with their own destructive ideas due to the deception of their minds, blaming others, resulting in intense anger. This in turn leads to unfounded hate, and finally culminates in acts of violence that may lead to the deaths of many innocent people.

WHAT LED TO THIS SYNOPSIS?

It was a walk-through of heaven, earth, and hell from 1960 to the present, the 22nd century, that caused this reflection and the uncovering of all that was seen. The search for the handling of spiritual experiences began the walk that resulted in uncovering the annihilation of nations that were taking place. One would expect that the primary source of spiritual understanding and guidance would be found in those dedicated to the service of God, ministers, bishops, priests, and other spiritualists. But that was not the case during those years. Very few existed and could not readily be found. Because of such a void, it was a most challenging journey to take. But God has a purpose for everything in each person's life, as with this journey, in which so much was revealed.

REVEALING THE ANNIHILATION OF NATIONS

WHY WAS IT SO DIFFICULT TO FIND IN-DEPTH SPIRITUAL GUIDANCE FROM GOD'S MINISTERS DURING THIS TIME PERIOD from the 1960s to now, 2022 or in more years to come?

Unknown to most of the average citizens in all nations, the world was caught up in the tremendous whirlwind of forces and ideologies that attempted to covet selfish and evil methods that fed into each other in the grooming of the minds of humans to destroy the spiritual essence and free will given by God to every human being. It was all planned in the early 1800s where one day if all went well, Humanism was to overtake God as the center of life. It was also predicted that this subversion would be routed through a council.

BELIEF SYSTEM

The plan of warfare to destroy the unity, goodness, and peace of a nation, or the world for that matter, is to aim at the nation's belief system, primary its religious belief. **Destroy the Faith of a nation from Within and then edge outward!** And at this time, the strength of the world was religion, especially the magisterium of the Catholic Church. Other ideologies latched onto this, and the annihilation of nations was in the making.

In doing research, besides interviewing people, I also came across writings that immediately connected to my experiences. The need to confirm them came strongly to the forefront. Much of the following facts are found in issues of The Fatima Crusader (FC) from The Fatima Center (FC) in different volumes and other sources listed in their References.

This grooming of destruction in all aspects of life was embedded from within. The period of interest up to the present was seen to have taken root way before in the 1800s, with its awareness to the Catholic Church throughout the years from 1820 to 1958. Its growth increased more so after World War II, especially during the 1940s, 1950s, and 1960s, when communism was on the rise after being fed by freemasons and Marxists. Key elements of diabolical destruction stemmed from:

ALTA VENDITA by John Vennari, FC p.1-4,12-13,16-17

FREEMASON-ALTA VENDITA written as a Masonic blueprint for the

subversion of the Catholic Church:

to destroy and infiltrate it under the disguises of modernism (subjectivity), liberalism (ambiguity), and progressivism (humanism embedded in radical liberalism), yet appearing so Apostolic and Holy in order to carry out and further its hidden agenda.

This secret document was written over 100 years ago, yet its writers were fully aware that it would take a long time to accomplish this, and certainly not during their lifetime. Some of its steps were:

-move beliefs regarding the doctrines and the teachings of Christ of the religious and lay people, from under the disguise from the spiritual to humanism, yet having them believe that they are still faithful and staunch Catholics

-groom and infiltrate the training of the upcoming priests, bishops, and cardinals in these areas so that a pope will emerge from them that will promote progressivism to the fullest.

-the terms such as enlightenment, renewal, and ecumenical would be used as a cover-up.

Pope Gregory XVI, Pope Pius the IX, X, XI, and XII fought against these subversive trends.

MARXIST

Before 1917, Russia was undergoing changes with Marxist ideas to change the world into a classless society. In its inception, it sounded so great but unfortunately, this class-less society was not one of equality for all. It was to be ruled by a government that would suppress anyone who was in disagreement with any of its rules, laws, or orders. The lives of individuals would have no value.

-People were no longer allowed to worship God or even conduct religious services, movement of atheism and religious indifference.

-any denial of a state order was met with fear, being arrested, rigid suppression, interred, and violence - fascism.

Total authoritarianism was promoted and in essence, freedom of the will given by God Almighty was removed from all human citizens

-traditions from the past were annihilated
-ownership by the government, capital, and products. No one could own private property, an element of humanistic socialism.

-marriage was just considered a public registry, its sanctity in Holy Matrimony being extinguished.

Crusade Magazine, P.O. Box 341, Hanover, PA 17331 September/October 2017 p.12

COMMUNISM A book titled The Naked Communist, states the communist goals along with the promotion of Marxism. Here are some: FC 123 p.22, 2018

-break down morality with the promotion of pornography, books, magazines, motion pictures, TV, and radio

-Destroy families by promoting promiscuity, masturbation, and divorce

-break up the safe world of children, raise them away from parental influence

-Change the outlook of homosexuality, degeneracy, and promiscuity as normal, natural, and healthy.

Besides the **Masons,** at the end of 1917, after **Marxist wanted to rule a class-less world,** the stage was set for Russia's **Communist** leader, Vladimir Lenin. Russia began to enslave its people under communism. He also set a plan in action to subvert Western civilization with Marxist and communistic ideas= Marxist/ Communism. It was to **use infiltration to destroy the catholic church, its leaders, clergy, and the faith of its people under destructive auspices that would appear to be holy and religious.**

Modernism - the subjective rules over the objective; man over God. A pamphlet from The Fatima Center titled Genuine Mercy & Counterfeit Compassion, states it clearly that instead of healing the wound of the sinner in granting reparation, support, and assistance, emphasis is tending only to the hurt feelings of the sinner. Emotions override the intellect and reason. Secular humanism.

Pope Pius the X fought against this as it shoved natural law, scholastic philosophy, and theology into the shadows. FC 117 p.43, 2016 However, it proved to be a useful weapon for communism. At this point, situation ethics came to the forefront without much clarity. As a result, Pope Pius XII condemned this as the subjective overruled the objective moral law that results from Natural Law and God's Will. FC117 p. 40 Rightfully so, as all energies, without profound spiritual thought, were geared towards humanity and not the uplifting of the soul/spirit to move the person towards God and heaven.

DESTROY FROM WITHIN BEGINNING WITH THE CHURCH, THE FAITH, AND VALUES OF CATHOLICS AND CHRISTIANS

FC 123 p. 15-16, 38,39, 2018 Bella Dodd, a catholic who turned communist and re-converted back to Catholicism under the influence of Bishop Fulton Sheen, revealed the following: that she, herself, sent more than 1,000 young men into the catholic seminaries during the 1930s and 1940s to break apart the church from within in order to vanquish the Faith of the people. It was an extremely successful move that stunned even the Kremlin. By the 1950s, as she continued on, many of these communist infiltrators were in the highest position within the Church, ready to break the Church apart so that it would change to adopt communist and atheist goals, secular humanism, and the indifference to various religions. The Revelations of the Holy Face of Jesus, The Fatima Center, www.fatima.org

In the meantime, the Marxist/ Communist movement to conquer the world went head-strong throughout other countries across the globe. On October 1, 1949, China became a communist country, although smaller sectors of it have existed since 1921. Others followed: Viet Nam-1954, Cuba-1959, Laos-1975, and North Korea was also in the thick of it. Presently, ISIS, the Taliban, Afghanistan, and Syria are all floundering over one another. Look up communist countries on google.

As previously stated, according to Bella, in the 1950s, many of the communist young men that infiltrated Catholic seminaries were bishops and in the upper echelons of the Catholic Church.

A council was to be called by Pope Pius XII to combat this movement, but due to his age and the insurmountable task it endured, he left it up to the next pope. It was a tragic decision as it fell into the hands of the subversive movement. The next pope was caught in its grooming efforts for progressivism. Pope John XXIII was elected.

DESTROY THE FAITH OF PEOPLE THROUGH THE CHURCH

"And there was war in heaven: Michael and his angels fought against the dragon, and the dragon fought and his angels, and prevailed not; neither was their place found anymore in heaven. And the great dragon was cast out, that old serpent, called the Devil, and Satan, which deceiveth the whole world: he was **cast out into the earth," (where humans would live),** "and his angels were cast out with him." REVELATION 12: 7-9

VATICAN II COUNCIL-RELIGIOUS BELIEFS

PRE-COUNCIL 1960

The Freemasons, Marxists, and communists inflamed with excessive lust for power laced with other capital vices went about in undercurrents and manipulative movements in carrying out their plans to destroy the Catholic Church and Nations around the world for their World Government. Simultaneously, Christians and non-Christians awaited the coming of the Vatican II Council with much curiosity, joy, and hope. To many believers, it was a beam of light to update the church in the teachings of Jesus Christ to the Reality of the World, and in clarifying areas in the Bible that were written in the essence of biases of cultures as well as personal agendas of the writers. Examples are creation and science in reference to earth and humans, especially the fall of humankind, along with the damnation of souls.

We are aware of the wonderful etymological style used in some of the writings in the Bible which simply express in some fashion the strong relationship between God and humankind within the context of an event. However, reality is deeply hidden and only somewhat expressed.

Creation

There is so much scientific evidence of creation, that shows the power of God, that God is Science, and the Creator of all things, even Mother Nature, that at times falls asleep. There have been so many theories and debates and disagreements over the inception of creation, between concepts as when looking at the biblical account of creation and the science of atoms, its protons, and electrons besides cosmic particles. Presently, there is so much evidence that shows how atoms can combine and rearranges their electrons and protons to regroup and form various forms of existence. We are aware also of many cosmic energies that come into play along with these processes.

Many ideas in agreements and disagreements regarding the beginning of the universe and the Creation of life and non-life have also been exchanged. Early philosophers looked at the 4 main elements in existence, earth, wind force, fire-heat, and water, and attributed Creation to the universe and all that is in it to one element or more. Different concepts also took place between philosophers like Aristotle and others and theologians and saints such as Thomas Aquinas.

However, Reality does not lie. Understanding that the biblical account of Creation took place in 7 days was written in an etymological style. It would not then contradict the scientific Reality of the formation of the universe and earth in perhaps being over 13 billion years old and the endless millenniums needed for the Creation of matter and life instead of 7 days. Looking over the Eras from the Pre-Cambrian Era to the Cenozoic Era, from the Age of Marine Invertebrates to the Age of Mammals, each scientific unit or unit of time can be assigned to a specific day in the biblical account of Creation in 7 days.

Moreover, because Science is reality and the workings of God's plan, Darwin's Theory of Evolution, along with the population of the homo sapiens by 10,000 BC and the similarity of tails in primates and humans, again does not contradict God's creation of reality. The power and spiritual beauty of God come into play with the infusion of the human soul and the degrees of consciousness in all matter and energy that is created.

Also, unlike the Biblical account regarding 4,000 years of human civilizations, the reality is, Science has found fossil remains and other evidences that date human civilizations back to Mesopotamia and the Sumerians over 5,000 years ago. In America, human remains have been found, dating back to 11,500 years ago. As Science keeps on finding evidences, the wonderment of God's Creation is revealed to us.

But all creation is under a divine guidance and power, a most pure spiritual plane way beyond cosmic energy that has it under control. It is how we handle our spiritual warfare as we pass through earth and not misuse or overuse all that is created for us that determines whether we help to keep things under control or not.

Right now, the vital signs of the earth are deteriorating rapidly, which can also annihilate nations. Earth's magnetic forces are moving and weakening in some global areas. This affects the earth's magnetic pulse. Fires on earth and the saturated regions with solar panels are killing birds in the air. Artificial light and artificial intelligence are affecting animals and humans alike. Climate change, if not controlled, will prove to be more disastrous than the present. It is now time to act for the sake of all humans on earth, ourselves, children, grandchildren, great-grandchildren, and future generations. All life should also be cared for, including animals, plants, and even the elements of fire, water, air, earth, and other planets.

Gender Bias

Many writings in the Bible have ties with various cultures. The etymological writing of the creation of male and female is the result of culturally patriarchy-biased practices that put the male above the female-gender bias. Many cultures latched on to this due to pride, an unhealthy one. Look around you, and you will surely see this.

Let us refer to something similar, which came first, the chicken or the egg? This fits in the reality of the process of evolution, the coming to be of male and female in unison, and the balance and equality of a certain species.

The Biblical account states that God created Adam, and then his rib was used to bring forth Eve. One is not better than the other because both came from the same source and are therefore equal. As Father Christopher K. preached, both are needed to support each other with love, respect, and kindness, spiritually, emotionally, and physically. The physical strength of the male and female complements one another. The female loses some strength monthly and in childbirth, especially in nutritional health. In support of each other in many instances, besides when propagating the human species, the stronger physical strength of the male is needed to help and support the female. Both continue in mutual support of each other in the rearing of their children together.

However, besides the account of Creation, gender equality was manipulated, as seen in Paul's (who was once a Jew) and Timothy's pieces of work. The respect that Jesus treated and showed to women, is not shown in some of the writings in the Bible. Because the biblical account put the male to be created first, then blamed the woman first for the original sin, and later males were called to follow Christ, some writers took advantage of this and in a culture, biased intent, put the male on a pedestal to be served and not one to support the female. The female was diminished with such a choice of words as a servant, slave, and silent as if she was not of the human race. Not once did Jesus ever demean women as such. Women were looked upon with respect as with His Holy Mother.

Original Sin

Another culturally biased area of interest to clarity was the truth and correction related to original sin. The etymological account of it in the Bible reveals that God gave Adam the command not to eat the fruit of a tree. The serpent tempted Eve, who believed and was captivated with what was said to her, and by the freedom of the will, ate of the fruit. She then gave the fruit to Adam, who was standing by her, to eat it. When confronted by God on their actions, Adam, without hesitation, turns around to blame Eve fully, who, in turn, blames the serpent.

Looking at this account in the Bible, it appears that only Adam was given the commandment directly from God not to eat the fruit from the tree of the knowledge of good and evil, for Eve was not yet created. However, Eve seemed to know of this order from God, perhaps from Adam. In the serpent's plan to destroy the right to heaven for humankind, it had to deaden Adam. And the way to do it was through Eve.

So, when tempted by the serpent (probably captivated with the sweetness of the pleasures of the 7 capital sins), Eve was deceived. Thinking and being assured by the serpent that there would be no harm, no death, she gave in to the pleasures of the temptation. Adam, although standing next to her, did not stop her. Seeing all with clarity, Adam knew the truths of its sinfulness and witnessed its results upon Eve, who first gave in being deceived. Adam was not deceived as Eve was. He had full knowledge of what was to be and, with his own free will, chose to sin. Question: was he aware of the stench of the vapors of the seven capital sins? When their actions were exposed by God, Adam turned to blame Eve entirely.

Genesis 2,3 The Gideons International, P.O. Box 140800, Nashville, TN 37214-0800 or www.gideons.org.

"Also, Adam was not deceived, but the woman was thoroughly deceived and came to be in transgression. However, she will be kept safe through childbearing, provided they continue in faith and love and sanctification along with soundness of mind." Timothy 2:14-15 And yet, the woman was blamed heavily.

This blind satanic pride of the male being first in everything and being put on a pedestal by writers with hidden agendas have been used for ages and never corrected. Misogamy against women is a result of the misuse of the teachings of Christ. In December of 2021, a news clipping recorded Pope Francis stating that the domestic violence against women is so high that it is somewhat satanic. Would not one think that perhaps the portions in the books of the Bible that are heavily laden with cultural biases that overtake the teachings of Christ should be brought to the attention of readers, pointed out in the homilies in church services, or simply change the terminology used to update its true meaning? One would hope that this is why Church Councils convene, or at least we hope it does.

In addition, Eve, because of her love for Adam- took all the blame and admitted such to God. This account was edited by Rutherford H. Platt, Jr. in 1927, The Forgotten Books of Eden, Bell Publishing Company, New York, 1981 edition, Adam and Eve Chap. V.: 4-5

Where is their accountability in all of this? Both Adam and Eve are to be blamed equally. Yet none of this has been addressed for all ages.

Souls Condemned

Unsettling concerns at that time, to mention a few, were also related to the well-intended honest errors of churches forbidding the cremation of bodies after death, condemning souls to hell that needed help and not damnation, such as souls that committed suicide when they called out for help, and no help was given, and the condemnation of mothers to death, without any say on her part or that of her husband when the choice was between saving the mother or the unborn child at childbirth. It was always taught that all suicide souls go to hell, that all mothers should die, and that cremation was forbidden.

Yet we know that decisions concerning souls belong only to God alone and not humankind. However, a few changes came way later, after much suffering by souls.

How can repentance be made for honest errors? Besides prayers and penance, it is known that Gregorian masses can be offered, 30 masses in 30 consecutive days to release souls that need help. Who would or should offer this up to the Lord?

There is no doubt that the purpose of the church on earth is to preach and teach what Jesus Christ taught us, to support all souls, including themselves, in the warfare of the reality of life on this earth as they fight alongside with all and help all souls to heaven. In so doing, damnable diabolical actions/behaviors that lead to the eternal hell, which the fallen angels rejoice in, can be pointed out to warn souls to avoid such and turn their lives around while they can. The love of God is to help us, especially when it comes to decisions that can only be made between the soul and God, not the church or the government. The soul rests in God's hands.

However, in the midst of all the revelry and excitement, the congregations of all denominations of religions were looking forward to what was to come with the Vatican II Council. This was because all Christian believers would be affected in some way in the practice of their faith. And it was hoped that the outcomes would increase one's faith and move the souls closer to God Almighty. Almost all believers looked forward to changes that would increase their love of God and be able to be saturated with His Divine Love. No one wanted changes that would become secular, worldly, progressive, or humanistic. Rather, believers had faith in the church leaders with hope and trust to advance the church and all believers through changes that would support bringing and increasing faith in The Reality of Life on Earth for God Almighty. They were not interested in laws, rituals, and doctrines that were made with hidden agendas, pride, gender biases, cultural biblical interpretations, and the like.

Unfortunately, the spiritual essence that so many yearned for was somewhat replaced with all that was secular, worldly, progressive, and humanistic.

This is somewhat of what happened when the books of the Bible were chosen. There were arguments, debates, and hidden agendas. The books chosen contains most of the essence of what God wants of us. Other books not chosen contain information that might bring more answers to what is in wonderment. Yet, the Holy Spirit is very important when reading Scripture in order to remove biases, gender inequity, racist interpretations, and the like.

The Third Secret of Fatima

Pope John XXIII opened the letter containing the third secret of Fatima in 1959, which was to be revealed to the entire world in 1960. The warning from the Mother of Jesus was given to the representatives of Her Divine Son on earth. It warned of tremendous upheavals and the insurrection and destruction of the church that could come from within, among other revelations. However, Pope John XXIII denied the request of Mary Immaculate and did not reveal the third secret of Fatima to the world, surpassing it and stating it did not concern his Pontificate at that time. FC 127 Summer 2021 p.11 Perhaps he was becoming overburdened due to movements that needed to occur in updating and moving the church forward besides dealing with factions of discord and personal agendas of others.

VATICAN II COUNCIL 1962-1965

The Vatican II Council began in 1962 and the communist seminarians were now priests, monsignors, bishops, and cardinals. The stage was set. And as stated earlier, some cardinals in Vatican II were masons. The elected and groomed Pope, knowingly or unknowingly, was in place to promote their efforts.

Unfortunately, it seems that he had no time to fully prepare for what was ahead. When the Vatican II Council opened, it was hijacked from him immediately from stronger progressive groups within, his cardinals, some of who were masons, FC 123 Autumn 2-018 p. 14, bishops, and priests.

A **Vatican-Moscow agreement** was made the evening before Vatican II Council was opened by a few Church leaders. This agreement assured that Communism would not be condemned so that Russian Orthodox participants could attend the Council. The news media informed the nation and world of their attendance.

Unknowingly, 450 bishops had requested that the Council papers and petitions include a **strong condemnation of Communism.** This was deliberately held back, and it never reached the Council Fathers. Furthermore, no clarity was given, and the reason of those who supposedly deceived the faithful and their Council Cardinals were never brought to light. FC The Revelations of the Holy Face of Jesus, John Vennari p.42

Clarification in simple terms would have brought some desperately needed understanding. The Church does condemn Communism but does not condemn the individual. Vatican II was to bring all of humankind together towards God Almighty. In so doing, and under such an agreement with Russia, the Russian Orthodox were able to attend the Council.

Moreover, Pope John XXIII strived to bring Peace to the world. On his 80th birthday, in November of 1961, Russia's Chairman Khrushchev sent him greetings which the Pope graciously accepted. A year later, allowing the Russian Orthodox participants to attend and observe the Vatican II Council under such an agreement, resulted in the creation of a trusting relationship between Russia and the Vatican.

Soon after the opening of the Vatican II Council in 1962, the news media blasted throughout the world, that Russia was already building missile sites in Cuba, creating an insurmountable threat to the United States of America and the world. Because of the trust that was built between the Vatican and Russia, Pope John knew that he needed to be involved for the sake of humankind. He communicated with President John Kennedy and Chairman Khrushchev and pleaded for peace, and world peace.

Result: Russia removed its missiles from Cuba and President Kennedy shared his gratitude with Chairman Khrushchev. Lawrence, Elliott. I Will Be Called John, A biography of Pope John XXIII. Reader's Digest Press, E.P. Dutton & CO. INC., New York 1973, pgs. 306-308.

And Chairman Khrushchev remained a communist, and Pope John remained a Catholic. Lesson learned?

Prayer to St. Michael the Archangel-One of the grave missteps taken by the Vatican II Council was

- **Removing the prayer of St. Michael, the Archangel** from the ending of every Holy Mass.

This was a very unfortunate move as it paved the way and opened the gates for diabolical changes to take place. Earth is where all the fallen angels were cast down.

Vatican II, purposely or not, made it easy for changes to occur on earth without heaven's protection.

St. Michael is the protector of all police officers and first responders as well, besides all who call upon his intercession to God the Father, Jesus the Son, the Holy Spirit, and the Mary Immaculate. Look at what is happening in 2021-22 with our police forces. Moreover, look at the tremendous increase of violence that is happening.

Ecumenism, dialogue, renewal-modern, words that were used to open the Council, so inviting yet could also be deceptive. All religions were made to be seen as acceptable as they all would lead to God, our common goal. And that is good that they all lead to God. Because humans are individuals, some need different channels to reach out to God.

However, in this move, the Divinity of God Almighty and the foundation of the Apostolic Catholic Church were not outwardly clarified or defended as well as the co-redemptive role of the Blessed Mother. The One, Holy, Catholic, and Apostolic Church began to plunge downward and be watered down. As with change, confusions result. However, it was later brought up and clarified in the Catechism of the Catholic Church in 1994. Some leaders saw where we were heading, and in the midst of upheaval, dissention, and the like, they held fast to try to gear the Church back on the path that it should be on.

Inculturation of religions, some examples:

Russian Orthodox do not accept the Immaculate Conception in a united manner, the papacy, and other truths of the Catholic religion. Their loyalty is to the Russian government-Sergianism. FC Issue 120, Autumn 2017

The majority of Protestants do not accept the Mother of God as the mother of men or her state of virginity.

Mohammedans, Jews, Hindus, and Buddhists reject the Immaculate Conception, her state of virginity, or as our Holy Mother. FC The Revelations of the Holy Face of Jesus, John Vennari p.46

Muslims-Islamic sources consist of the following: Quran-Mohammad's revelations, Hadith-Quran's commentaries and oral traditions with Mohammand, and Sira-Mohammand's biography. Muslims believe only in Allah, the Creator, Jesus only as a human messenger, thereby lacking divinity and denying any incarnation, and Mary, as the mother of Jesus.

Therefore, the suffering of the crucifixion, death, and resurrection of Jesus is denied. And the **jihad, known as the holy war, is to have Islam rule on a worldwide basis.** The Fatima Center, "Fatima, Islam, and Our Lady's Coming Triumph", Matt Gaspers, Canada BT055 pgs. 10-15,17

Luther- He believed in God. That is all. In his 1517 revolt against the catholic church, he attacked and denounced the Papacy. The Holy Mass was also condemned in his view. As for the Bible, that is all that he held worthy of belief, denying God's ministers the right to interpret Sacred Scripture. Yet he, himself, meddled in its interpretation, preaching that only faith alone will save a person, and that good works are not needed, contrary to the teachings of St. Paul's Letter to the Romans and The Epistle of James. He also rejected the Book of Revelation and the Ten Commandments and approved of sex sins and promoted cruelty to the poor people under the disguise of defending them. FC 112. Winter 2016 pgs. 30-32 Pope John Paul II praised Luther for his "deep religiousness." FC 116 Autumn 2016 p. 32

What happened was a positive approach to respecting all religions in their pathways to God, but also in contrast, a deliberate opposition to the Holy Trinity and the role of the Mother of God as a Co-redeemer. Some previously groomed members of the Vatican II Council took on a laxed attitude in its foundation of faith which fed into the communist goal towards atheism through the weakening of religion.

Vatican II Changes in the Church

In the meantime, with some confusion and precarious arrows of uncertainty heading their way, many Christians tried to adjust to the changes both positively and negatively. Some areas affected were their church doctrines, rules, forms of worship in services and facilities, management, and other areas. Some are listed here with a few wonderments from many believers:

- **Removing the Prayer to St. Michael the Archangel** at the ending of every Mass that asked for his interception to God for our protection against all evil, especially from all the fallen angels, demons, and devils.

Was a new prayer being drawn up to replace this one?

- **Options to say the Apostles Creed** that contains the truths of the Catholic religion, and the Nicene Creed were given.

- **Women no longer need to wear any hat** or veil on their heads when attending the Holy Mass.

This was a good change to reality from what was written in the Bible, as God does not judge by the hair or hat on a person's head, but by the soul of a person. However, the freedom to choose to wear such was an option given to all.

A woman shared how she was belittled when she wore her cultural attire to Mass one Sunday. That was all she had and could afford. The priest from the pulpit stated that she should wear her Sunday best only. He failed to see that not all people could afford the Western Sunday best.

- **The ringing of the bells at Consecration**, a gesture of reverence and holiness, recognizing the high and intense spiritual presence of the Lord was removed.

This helped to put the soul into deep meditation with the Lord God. Presently, some churches are bringing it back.

- **Sacrament of the Holy Eucharist-Holy Communion can now be administered by lay people.** This was a form of community and the involvement of the laity. However, some would raise it so high that the receiver had to cut off their meditation with the Lord in order to recognize it is lifted so high.

- **Holy Communion can now be received in one's hands** besides the tongue, and fasting can be limited to one hour before its reception.

- The consecrated wine into **the blood of Christ was now given with the same cup to all** who partook of it. Any thought for health issues?

A person with blood disease just wanted to dip his sacred host into the chalice so that no one would get his disease. He was told that he could not do so and had to drink from the cup. He left the altar without the Blood of Christ.

- **After receiving the sacred host, all had to remain standing** till the last person received. Respecting being in union with others at this point took over the meditation a soul was having with the Lord.

- **Everyone held hands** during Mass with the prayer to Our Father

Any thought for health issues? Because of COVID 19, many just hold the hands of family members.

- **Greetings** are given before Mass, and again during Mass in some churches. Reason?

- **Sacrament of Extreme Unction** for the sick and dying were given in Masses

- **Baptism was** now done in Masses.

- **Holy Mass, in order to be meaningful to the congregation, was initiated by Pope John Paul II to be said in English and many othe cultural languages.** At one point, Latin was allowed for those who wished to have it, who understood it. However, it is now forbidden. No choice is available for those who wish to attend a Mass in Latin, a language that many studied in high schools. Why is this as even the Pope speaks in his language when he says mass and we can't understand it?

- **Baltimore Catechism has been changed to the Catechism of the Catholic Church in the early 90s.**

Much thought and well intentions went into its revision, a very good revision especially as written in the Compendium, Catechism of the Catholic Church 2006. However: Some deep theological thinking may need to be addressed, for example, in the area of eschatology.

1. **When the lives of a mother and baby are at stake at childbirth,** a decision long ago was made by men who did not understand childbirth and the fragility of some women's bodies, made not by doctors, nor the parents of the child, etc. that sent many mothers to their deaths. This is a decision that should be only between the parent and God.

2. **All suicide souls were also condemned to hell** via church teachings and beliefs.

3. **Cremation was also forbidden.**

4. **Capital punishment** is an area not of the church but of the justice system on earth as allowed by God provided it is of justice, not with racism, or white supremacy, or judges and prosecutors and attorneys that are politically appointed for personal agendas. In a democratic society, it is a system of fairness, diversity with respect, and dignity in relation to the insights of the Constitution, highly ethical in its decision for all people, not a few.

Perhaps the church can now repent for its mistaken condemnation to hell, of all suicide souls of long ago and all the mothers that were sent to their deaths, more so, if unwillingly.

However, after almost 30 years after Vatican II, the church now addresses rightfully the state of suicide souls that were not given the help when in time of need. This is a positive step forward in living in the World of Reality with God.

And now, in 2022, many funerals with cremation occur. Another step forward is living in Reality with God.

The rightful place of capital punishment must now be addressed by an ethical, non-racist, and non-politicalized Judiciary Branch.

- **Sacrament of Penance** - General absolution was and is given in some churches.

- **Sacraments of First Communion (Holy Eucharist) and Confirmation** are now given at the same time.

At one time the Sacrament of Confirmation was prepared through the church and if a student attended a catholic school, preparation was done there. With Vatican II, it moved only through the church to promote community. As result, some students who did not attend the additional classes in religion outside of classes in a Catholic school did not receive the Sacrament of Confirmation. Only in 20221-22 did the change come about where now at First Holy Communion, Confirmation is now administered. This step was very positive. Now the question is how does the church make up for those students who lost their opportunity while they attended a Catholic School after Vatican II? How to restart the desire to move to this sacrament with all of the disruptions that have taken place in their lives?

- **Community and collective time were stressed.**

Everything was now done in a communal fashion so that besides sports, parish time also ruled over family time. This also was done in other religions. Did families have time alone to communicate just with their family members, to discuss family issues in private, and to bond and learn how to support one another?

- **Deacons** now assist priests at Mass.

Understandably if there is a shortage of priests. In addition, it included the laity to be part of the church rituals.

- **Girls are now altar girls, besides having altar boys. Also, women are now collectors** of donations during masses as well as men, still somewhat subservient but a good start in a community concept. This was also a move towards gender/ laity equality within the church.

Finally in 2022, nuns and lay women could also hold positions within the Vatican. Why did it take from 1962 to 2022? Just a thought, but a positive move.

- **Church altars faced the congregation with their furniture rearranged. Statues were moved to** the shadows of its church walls as Catholics were accused by others that they worshipped these statues. These non-Catholics failed to see the connection between pictures of loved ones and statues, as reminders. Some churches had the courage, and the fortitude to keep the holy statues as reminders in place.

- Nuns, Priests, and Brothers can forego the traditional religious habit and dress as the ordinary layperson.

Saint Padre Pio reminded a priest to always dress as a priest, and not as a lay person.

Some went to the extreme. A husband felt so distraught as he listened to a religious now wearing gold chain necklaces, who shared how she now goes to a weekly hairdresser appointment. He could only afford to send his wife to the hairdresser once every six weeks, and certainly, no gold chains to wear. Yet, there were many religions that kept their vows of poverty and continued to be in the service of God with simplicity.

- Situation Ethics, a very compassionate move, became activated without the clarity needed for it to function in a spiritual sense. As a result, it fell into human satisfaction as it was being used and misused especially in the areas of divorces and homosexuality. Situation ethics is compassion with mercy, and certainly helps souls with God's understanding, but should be applied only in the grave or serious circumstances when deeming such a decision. And in some instances, when it becomes only between God and the soul, the church should offer all the spiritual support it can give to that soul. Some priests have executed it in such a manner, and this is good.

Situation Ethics as it should be in relation to abortion and other areas related to procreation must be distinguished between:

Those souls in innocence, those in their spiritual relationship with God and with vows taken with God as their witness

And be separated from:

The souls that are willingly involved in the destructive abuse and violence among humans with non-spiritual intent such as sex

trafficking, prostitution, drug abuse, and violence among males and females.

Laws and consequences should apply to these areas of abuse and violence among humans that destroy one another endlessly, involving males and females.

DESTROY THE FAITH AND VALUES OF PEOPLE THROUGH EDUCATION

SENSITIVITY TRAINING AND ENCOUNTERS

Within the middle and latter part of the 1960s, sensitivity training and encounters related to Marxists and Communist goals towards the control of a world government, began to flood from the college level to the training of the faithful. This had already infiltrated and was taking place in catholic seminaries with upcoming religious. People, who included the faithful and catholic school teachers, were grouped and encountered one another with the intent of releasing all of their inhibitions all under the disguise of professional training in **EDUCATION** and moving with the **renewal of the church**. You were free to touch one another's body, anywhere that you wanted to. You were free to say whatever you wanted to with the freedom of any tone of voice or even choice of words, including swear words. Trying to teach freedom from being uninhibited led to a lack of self-control, lack of human dignity, and lack of respect for self and your neighbor. It was also ok to lie and not have to tell the truth. It became me, myself, and I training in a very abusive form.

Moving away from values and so-called norms was in the making. To be a good Christian was looked upon to be outdated as time went on. Holy purity in life along with fidelity and faithfulness in marriage was being torn apart. The narcissist attitude, and the misuse of me, myself, and I psychology were being spread across the board. Atheism with the questioning of the existence of Our Lord Jesus Christ was moving in a manipulative undercurrent manner. A community of such thinking was being developed also in the **FAMILY** with the intent to deliberately destroy the sanctity of marriage and remove children from the control of their parents. And this training was also incorporated in **BUSINESS, and MILITARY sectors** as well as other organized careers.

This movement, which was very well planned, was intended to attack and weaken the church. It was a precursor to the sexual revolution that was to run rampant in no time at all assisted by drug abuse which would then weaken the family and society. It would further lead to the eventual takeover of the Democratic government that held America together. Unpleasantly, the stench of some people on the far right that were influenced or groomed in freemason/ Marxist, and communistic ideologies, lingered in the air of freedom, fairness, and safety that covered America.

Progressivism- a form of radical Liberalism

Once again, I refer to Randy Engel's Rite of Sodomy, Vol. III Pgs. 563, 573 - 579. This report confirms all that occurred before the 1960 and forward, the changes that took place within the catholic church and the training of candidates in the seminaries moving away from Thomastic thinking to theology embedded in politics as a result of radical liberalism. It validates what we as catholic school teachers and others were confronted with and made to participate in, secular psychological indoctrination with encounter groups, sensitivity training, changes within the church, relativism or narcissistic lifestyle, and placing sexuality as the center of being.

Communism was moving well in tearing apart the super nation of the world, the United States of America from within, beginning with its stronghold, its religion, its faith in God, especially, the Roman Catholic Church. Other church denominations also followed suit in trying to modernize their practices as well.

But by saving graces from heaven, some church denominations kept their stronghold on the values from the teachings of Jesus Christ and did not buckle to progressivism. Some Catholic clergy, religious, nuns, and laity also held fast to the spiritual plane and basic articles of faith as stated in the Apostles Creed. Many of the faithful would not bend to the subversive efforts and held the hand of Jesus with a tight grip.

EDUCATIONAL AND PSYCHOLOGICAL TRENDS

In education, complementing Sensitivity Training was the misuse of the Values Clarification method, along with Maslow and Erikson's Psychologies.

Values Clarification was a clinical method wrongly implemented by the educational field. It allows a person to make a choice without being influenced by others. Educators took it and refrained from teaching students as to what was dangerous or good. No values were taught in catholic schools and public schools as well. The spiritual level of souls was being sorely neglected. God is good. And if goodness is not taught, God is not taught.

Maslow's psychology tending to the basic needs of humans, although very excellent, was so overly emphasized to draw religion to the human level, thereby neglecting the spiritual.

Erickson's psychology which tended to develop a healthy self-concept, and self-esteem, was used beyond what it was intended. Me, myself, and I self-concept rationales swung beyond its intentions and went gearing towards selfishness, thereby deliberately negating the needs and respect for others.

These manipulative abuses of good, solid, and healthy psychological methods misled the human mind towards selfishness and self-survival, not thinking of loving your neighbor as yourself, the second great commandment of God. It is also a very fast way to destroy democracy, that exists for the good of all.

ATTEMPTS TO COUNTERACT VARIOUS MISUSE TRENDS

Educational, affective, and moral development research studies were looked at in order to return values to the lives of humans. Unfortunately, during these decades, the counteractive forces somewhat overpowered these valuable studies. However, some were implemented by staunch educators where the institutional atmosphere would allow such.

William Purkey advocated for intentional inviting environments which would help students cope with meeting school expectations that would result in competence and school achievement.

Jack Canfield wrote a book on "100 Ways to Enhance Self-Concept in the Classroom."

Edward Deci is known for the great effort in the affective domain in moving extrinsic motivation (misuse of awards) to intrinsic motivation that would develop self-responsibility, competence, self-esteem, and autonomy vs. being controlled.

Madeline Hunter promoted instructional strategies that listed learning objectives, problem solving, immediate feedback, and mastery. Presently, this is seen in many aspects of education, instructions, and common core state standards.

Moral Development was so needed at this time. **John Dewey** postulated 3 levels of moral reasoning: preconventional-satisfaction of fundamental needs, conventional-standards of society, and postconventional-conscience. Paralleling along this line were **Kant**-Universals, **Piaget**-cognitive development, **Plato**-good/justice, and **Lawrence Kohlberg** with his six stages of moral development.

In a nutshell, Kohlberg's stages are:

Stage One: simple obedience or there will be punishment

Stage Two: satisfy your own needs; also learning the value of being reciprocal, if you do this, I will do that, etc.

Stage Three: group approval, good girl, good boy

Stage Four: recognize authority, rules, law

Stage Five: living in the community, respecting rights

Stage Six: Non bias, Human dignity for all

The author of this book, in conjunction with other moralists, agrees that **Mother Teresa** exemplifies the intellectual and moral development of Stage 7, Human Spirituality.

These attempts have helped to sustain the nation up to the present time, in the 21st Century, despite the counteractive forces that are still at play. The Inexoration of Character, Moral, and Citizenship Education in Public and Religious Educational Institutions, Dept. of Curriculum and Instruction, U. of H., R.S. 1989.

DESTROY THE MORALS OF PEOPLE, THEIR FAMILIES, AND SOCIETY

PORNOGRAPHY, MOVIES, SEXUAL REVOLUTION

Again, the stage was set with the freedom from inhibitions, with no values being taught by the church or schools, with self-gratification setting in.

Pornography

By around the late 1960 and middle 70s, **cable television** took over the sanctity of all households. Pornography, free sex, adultery, fornication, homosexuality, sex trade, servitude, prostitution, and sexual abuse spread so rapidly as prurient and salacious behaviors increased. Families were unprepared in dealing with such, feeling precarious with some of their efforts. Not one aspect of life was spared. This was coupled with other societal vices or evils such as the abuse of drugs.

Movies

Along with pornography entering into the homes via cable television, movies at theaters also joined in the money-making trend of aiming at human vices. Sexual intercourse among married couples, adulterers, and fornicators was and is seen in many movies, besides violence, drugs, and vomiting. Much older men were matched with very young women, the age of their own children or grandchildren across movie screens to draw more audiences per capital.

Children's movies, coloring books, and story books, with so much innocence and fantasy, even in cartoons, were rudely interrupted suddenly with an adult sexual innuendo or human vice within the movie, coloring book, storybook, or cartoon. This occurs even in online APPS of children's programs. It causes a quick crash upon the child's innocence and one can detect the initial grooming taking effect.

Sexual Revolution

The sexual revolution infiltrated the **CHURCH** with much sexual abuse in many forms, with its clergy, from cardinals, bishops, priests, and other religions, among themselves and with lay people of all ages and marital statuses. Up to the present time, 21st Century, some of the Popes did their very best to deal with this diabolical atmosphere in the midst of dismal stress factors within and surrounding the Church environment. However, many accused clergy were assigned to other parishes instead of being held responsible for their actions of sexual abuse, homosexuality, and promiscuity.

Tending to the healing of their victims was rashly neglected and voided especially with the use "of the statute of limitations." Movies, such as The Keepers, Spotlight-2015 Oscar-winning film, and many others, and an increased number of documentaries such as Procession, The Rite of Sodomy, Homosexual and the Catholic Church by Randy Engel, revealed how the destruction of a nation can occur through lack of its belief and value systems. Sadly, as time went on, clergy and religious left the Sacrament of Holy Orders and their religious vocations.

Other churches, such as the Southern Baptist Church, also had to deal with tremendous sexual abuse from among its pastors and other church personnel. Similarly, allegations were handled in a way to protect themselves and not be responsible to the victims. Star-Advertiser, 5-27-22, p. 8.

Many of those who should or could have helped souls seeking spiritual guidance, lacked the proper training on the spiritual level and were intertwined with the forces of change towards modernism that hid behind the words of ecumenism, holy, and renewal, within the church.

The sanctity of the **FAMILY,** the home, the basis of **Society,** was not spared. Marriages under the Sacrament of Holy Matrimony, even marriages bonded for 30 years and more, were broken as vows of fidelity, faithfulness, holy purity, and purity of heart were destroyed in the confusion and upheavals that deliberately occurred resulting in the human consumption of pleasures. The church was not much help here as she herself was going through the same revolution with sexual abuses from within. By the 1980s-90s, divorces due to adultery and infidelity increased abundantly including fornication, resulting in many single-parent homes. From 1960 to 1978, divorce rates soared from 5% to 20% along with illegitimate births. Homicides and suicides, along with school dropouts also increased tremendously. Source: National Center for Health Statistics, World Almanac, and Book of facts, 1983, U.S. Public Health Service.

Alongside of these happenings in addition to latchkey children, influences to human behaviors also resulted from studies done by Kinsey on male and female sexual behaviors, Freud's spare the rod, and Spock's independence vs. nurturing, and permissiveness in alignment with that of Rogers. The Inexoration of Character, Moral, and Citizenship Education in Public and Religious Educational Institutions, Dept. of Curriculum and Instruction, U. of H., R.S. 1989.

Because of broken marriage vows, children were no longer living under the care and love of both parents in one united household. Some children were co-parented, others were passed around to other family relatives, friends, and even strangers. And still there were children who were abandoned and the suffering of the innocent ones increased. As time passed on and due to circumstances, men and women began to choose to just live together without uniting under Holy Matrimony.

Wasn't this one of the Marxist goals? It is so easy to choose evil as a result of original sin. Where is God? Where is spiritual help? The seven capital sins ran and are running rampant.

The freedom to choose good is the result of having faith. And it is nourished with prayers.

MARXIST COMMUNIST GOALS TO DESTROY AND OVERTAKE A NATION CONTINUED

From here on in, it was easy to further attack and **destroy the faith** in one's Society. The gate was now open to increase the lessening of its value system through the use of drugs, racism, violence, devil worship in cults, negative or satanic psychic forces, subliminal music, and other vices that allow capital sins to enter. Portals to evil were opened, for example, with the use of the Ouija board.

Many living souls fell slaves to negative forces, while others did not know how to cope with such. Spiritual guidance was lacking as training for clergy to minister it was neglected in the seminaries. Very, very few clergies knew how to handle spiritual experiences. Ministers from other churches, as well as ordinary lay people, even some who lived in poverty but practiced living in a highly spiritual way of life, would step in to help and fill the spiritual void.

DRUGS

By 1970 the abuse of drugs seeped into the lives of people of all ages and in all vocations in society. This chemical abuse traveled rampart into the hands of elementary school children on to the high school level in religious and public schools where students were selling drugs to their classmates in the 1980s. What would one expect if following and misusing the values clarification method in teaching and not helping students to make valued sound decisions? Drugs were disguised as candy or hidden in playful tattoo papers for the young ones. Even cough medicines with alcohol content were used by teens and others.

Adults and teens gave in to these abusive addictions. The warping of minds that saw evil as good, and good as evil occurred especially with the highly addicted use of the drug-crystal meth, also known as ice. It removes the moral conscience of a soul. One highly addicted ice couple lost their home and lived in the pens with their pigs.

It also produces much fear and phobias that are not in reality, only in the mind of the addicted.

The use of fear is one of the communist goals to take control of a nation. It was in the news in the 1950-60s that the communist will try to take control of America through drugs and other subversive ways. In communist countries where its governments are authoritarian and rule by absolute authority, coercion, suppression of opposition, punishment, and violence are used to attain their goals. Drug addicts are arrested instead of being helped in healing centers.

Other drugs without any medical monitoring were used abundantly: cocaine, marijuana, and heroin. New drugs appeared and are still on the scene, ecstasy, date drugs, and others. This abuse of drugs keeps rocketing even today when pain killers such as hydrocodone, oxycodone, morphine, heroin, and even fentanyl are also added to the list.

The state of life and the happiness of individuals were and are swept away so easily. Murders, possession of guns by people who do not qualify to be in possession of such - age, background checks, etc., the finding of body parts in desolated areas, violence, the abuse of sex trafficking and prostitution, suicides, deaths due to drug overdose and stealing to keep up drug habits increased tremendously. Personal relationships, properties, families with drug-addicted unborn children result, and homes with their dreams of happiness were and are still being destroyed.

Opening Of Portals-An Increased Interest Followed

Peeking into psychic gifts, magic, fantasy, etc. sometimes starts off with curiosity, from the nudging of others for entertainment, as an interest, or just innocence. Unfortunately, no one was and is there to warn the individual of the dangers regarding portals that can be opened and be very difficult to close, and sometimes not at all by the individual. There were spiritual guides available; there were very few and difficult to find.

Psychics Those who are truly gifted by God Almighty can be detected in how they use their gift. They will use their gift in a salubrious manner, only to help souls in carrying their cross or crosses (which we all have) towards God. No payment is required, although some may allow one to volunteer to do so or not. One must use prudence also in the areas of seances.

Beware of those who lead souls astray from God, to depend on them alone and not God, that sucks and drains a person's energy, of the soul, mind, or body, or finances. These work along satanic ends in mind and aim to destroy the soul of a person.

Paranormal activities that can also open portals increased under the guise of being entertainment, or an area of interest. Very few clergy, ministers, or others spoke to warn individuals to cease from it for it shares the opened door for spirits to enter without God's permission. Again, the lack of training for clergy, ministers, and others is revealed. The book, Hauntings, Possessions, and Exorcisms by Adam C. Blai, fully explains about the danger of such spiritual encounters and is highly recommended for reading.

Games and fun books for adults and children also opened portals towards destruction. The Dungeons and Dragons game, if played properly, is a good game to play that includes all its members. However, if not followed properly, it can addict the minds of some players to live the game in reality and ruin their lives. Parents need to advise their children on what games are safe, and how to participate in games properly, including those in technology.

The use of the **Ouija Board** game became popular. Because it opens the portal to spirits without God's permission, it invites much **danger** to a person that can be disastrous. If it is an evil spirit, the player had no control over it. This dimension belongs only to God alone and humankind must not tamper or intervene in it.

The Ouija Board game is also combined at times with tarot cards. Some games are created as decorative wall hangings or even table cloths. Because these can open the gateways to the other portals, one must not tamper in this area.

Online games in technology should also be screened out by parents as it is one way to instantly twist the minds of innocence. This along with **coloring books**, and **apps** that draw children into their web of fantasy and fun with negative concepts hidden in their pictures which lead their minds towards the **dark side that desensitizes their minds to that which is diabolical,** need to be weeded out by parents.

Subliminal Music entered the scene in the 60s and continues to do so. Messages from such music embed into one's subconscious mind. Such techniques used are hearing words backward, having flashing lights between words, and hearing only the musical instruments with their moving beats that over-ride the hidden sensual words in the background. It embeds certain words that build on emotions and feelings and changes in behaviors, that gradually desensitize values in the mind, an easy way of brainwashing.

The whole system of society within the nation was dwindling as planned by the Freemasons, and Marxist/ Communist to secular communist humanism. It was being made ready for the picking! Religion and values were watered down as the spirit of the soul for God was no longer the center of belief. Changes within the Church and elsewhere were implemented without the necessary and clear and important explanations given, thereby causing tremendous doubt and confusion. Society that consisted of the families were destroyed, with children and adults being caught in the waves of sexual revolution along with no inhibitions in speech, thoughts, behaviors, pornography, drug abuse, and addiction, subliminal music, and the opening of portals that should remain close.

WHAT HELD THE NATION TOGETHER IN THE MIDST OF ALL THIS UPHEAVAL?

In the midst of these abundant and unforeseen upheavals of change, there were the holy clergy and religious ones, the priests and ministers of all church denominations who held on to their religious vows of Holy Orders or religious commitment to God who continued to preach the WORD. These warriors of God respected their commitment to celibacy, their vows of poverty, chastity, and obedience, and some still wore their religious habits as a reminder of their vows to themselves and to the laity that sacrifice and suffering for God are acceptable.

With negative words thrown at them or being taunted and attacked by and from other fellow clergies, religious, ministers, primarily those indoctrinated with progressive/liberalism or communistic foundations, and other so-called Christians, these dedicated humans with integrity got up after being knocked down many times and carried their crosses in the service of Our Holy Lord. These are the stronghold for God, the essence of all higher power, in all of the teachings of Jesus Christ. They are the powerhouse on this earth, for the laity and church congregations, and the public citizenry. They live the reality of the love of God, of truth, and maintain hope for all. Remember, the fallen angles also occupy this earth.

Unfortunately, some devout Christians left their churches of faith (exodus of Catholics and Christians) due to much confusion, some beginning to question and deny the reality of Jesus Christ or even God, thereby falling victims to the Communist teachings of atheism.

Devout Christians of all denominations on earth held on to their vows of Holy Matrimony with God as their witness. Keeping their vows of fidelity to one another, and supporting one another, provided the refuge that humankind was in dire need of at this time. Non-Christians also shared in this provision.

Children that were brought up in decent homes continued to learn human values, love for God, and respect for self and others. Importantly, many non-Christians are certainly included here, who held on to common sense human values that respect human dignity and the universal value of Goodness.

Interestingly, you dear reader, can possibly see how the upheavels and turmoils through the many years of changes gave birth and formed the diverse thinking, attitudes, and outlooks towards solving problems, education, dealing with society, etc. among the generations:

G.I. or Greatest Generation born 1901-24,
Silent Generation/Traditionalists born 1925-42,
Boom Generation born 1943-60,
Generation X born 1961-81,
Millennials born 1981-2001,
Generation Z listed as born 1996-2010, and
Generation Alpha born 2011-2025.

WHERE ELSE MUST DESTRUCTION TAKE PLACE IN ORDER TO ANNIHILATE A NATION?

DESTROY A NATION'S GOVERNMENT

By the year 2000, Freemason and Marxist/ Communistic ideologies of progressive liberalism continued to infiltrate nations throughout the world, and surprisingly, seemed to be quite successful in America. The infiltration in the 1930s of communists' seminarians in the Church to destroy values, the implementation in the 1960s of Sensitivity Training in the church, who in turn gave it to its schools, while along the line there was an outflow to businesses, and any area that was penetrable (where it is acceptable to say whatever you want to even though it is a lie, to touch, to release any inhibitions or self-control) merrily walked its pathway. The support of the drug trade and free sex that began to explode in the 1970s on, especially with the development of technology-cable television, the use of threats of violence as a method of control along with racism, were meeting the plan and goals of their instigators.

As the plan of destruction kept on its path, Churches and their congregations still emerged in confusion, and surprisingly, back in 1989, public education that adopted pedagogical areas which were misused came to the realization of the danger students and the future society were facing. As a consequence, they retrieved character education programs, for example, Guidance curriculums. However, society was still dismantled and many families were torn apart. Deaths, threats, and human abuses increased as respect, self-control, and love for thy neighbor disappeared into the shadows. With common sense, those of strong faith kept on the pathway of human integrity and decency.

On the American political scene, the infiltration of progressive liberalism such as freely shooting and carrying guns began to show its face by the year 2000. "Divided we fall," started to take place in an undercurrent within the government system of the United States of America. Two parties that once were united in protecting DEMOCRACY were more or less united before 2015 as seen in the platform of some political candidates.

THE BIG LIE

The 2016 election promoted the two American political parties to be at odds with one another. But not all were or are in disagreement inwardly. Negative forces such as lies that lead to bigotry, conspiracies, anger, hate, violence, greed, misuse of power, lack of self-control and inhibitions, and misogamy, were on the rise, and FEAR stopped many good politicians from speaking out to support our democratic government that was formed to be FOR and BY the people.

Fear is used to remove the freedom of choice "THE FREEDOM OF THE WILL TO CHOOSE GOOD", from individuals through the power of control. Political power when used in an unjust and diabolical manner, becomes a powerful agent of control and lust for power. Moreover, negative forces can easily destroy a nation and democracy.

Is this an area of the government that acts as a portal for any man of 666, or woman, to enter?

When the freedom of choice is removed due to coercive methods, it results in the neglect to fight for what is right, good, and decent. Further, it fails to uphold human dignity and peace for all of humankind. Most devastating, it is a great attempt to destroy our gift from God Almighty, to **choose well** when faced with evil.

Within the Bible, it clearly is seen that Satan is the father of all Lies, and the weapon that is used by all the fallen angels or devils is Fear. The armor of God is Faith without fear in the name of Jesus Christ who has come in the flesh-Truth.

The political platforms of the candidates for the next president of the United States of America in 2020 -21 exposed the disarray and deception of all segments of society. TV news channels as well as newspapers, magazines, and other media covered daily happenings that flooded the nation.

The separation of church and state was not being followed. One political candidate that promoted these negative forces, especially with a fraud election lie, simply had to add a pro-life stand to his platform (evil in the form of an angel of light) and this element of exploitation caused many ministers of God, especially those from evangelical churches with predominately white churchgoers to blindly back him up with the election fraud. New York Times. Little could be foreseen that once government controls you without your freedom to choose, then the next step could result in controlling your pro-life concept.

When this candidate was not elected, one minister cast it off as God was showing him humility. Might God also be showing the church to be humble and in need of correction too? Like all of us? No words were further given by churches via news media on a nationwide scale.

In 2021, my area of occupancy was composed of many Asian residents that had fled Communist China within the past two and three years. At one time, married couples in China could only have one birth male child-pro-life control. As time went by, married couples had to make a payment to the government to have a second child. Now there is no policy as a check and balance are missing in the system. This leads to corruption and greed with underlying resources such as drug dealings, gun sales, and underground powers running some government goals described as being bullish in nature.

Would America be heading this way?

On the other hand, the opposite political candidate that is a staunch catholic Christian with limitations and faults like everyone else, in promoting the dignity of humankind, was cast aside by ministers because of his pro-choice political platform, protecting the freedom of the will, the right to choose good. The separation of the church and state was not heeded by others. Instead, Bishops in America met in the fall of 2021 about the distribution of Holy Communion, and some considered withholding it from the elected president because he promoted God's will to allow us to choose freely, towards good. Even the Vice-President and others have been threatened with such regardless of their faith in God.

Politics has no place between a person's soul and God. When it is used as such, the church falls under its spell and both eventually destroy one another. Look at the history of the past when the papacy was involved in politics.

It is the divine duty of the ministers of God to preach, teach, and live pro-life so that when choices are to be made, by His gift of the FREEDOM OF THE WILL TO CHOOSE GOOD, Christians will rightfully choose pro-life. The ultimate choice a person makes is between God and that soul. And even if the church does not understand, it should still support the individual, for the choice that was made was done in the goodness in their relationship to God. He or she will have to live with their decision with God.

The rightful election of 2020 for a President of the United States of America was met with negative forces. Planned over a century ago by the freemasons, and then the Marxist/communists with their successful grooming, the perfect person to carry out their plan was the outgoing president. Because he believed and felt that he had the power and right to be president in opposition to the will of choice and votes of the people, being fully recalcitrant in belief and attitude, lies were stated to warp and cause doubt in people's minds against the proper election processes in place, **before** it even took place. A seed of evil was planted in the minds of constituents before the act of goodness even occurred.

If lies are repeated, minds that do not look into true facts start to believe the lies. Along with lies, deceit, fraud, insincerity, and prevarication, the use of courts, state legislatures, news media, the military, and other right extremist groups that were infiltrated by white supremacists groups (promotes hate, and recruits members through propaganda via the internet platforms), and Congress were employed to spread more lies and overturn his presidential defeat. This tremendous lust for power, control, and greed is overwhelming. Money was also raised by these groups. The Year In Hate 2020, Southern Poverty Law Center, Montgomery Al.

The political uniting of Supreme Court Judges, court judges, attorney generals, prosecuting attorneys, and others, resulted in similar minds that were to weaken the justice system and democracy. Criminals and perpetrators were being treated better than their victims in the court systems using their background as excuses-low socio-economic, lack of education, and other social misgivings. They and the courts portrayed blindness to the fact that they were killing their fellow human beings, destroying properties, and businesses that would provide jobs for their victims, and hurting citizens that could help them with their education besides putting others in the face of danger. Lawlessness was being favored over justice.

Fortunately, and with blessings from above, the democracy of America was upheld by those judges, attorney generals, prosecuting attorneys, lawyers, and others with great fortitude, prudence, and faith, regardless of their religion or even no religion but knew the value of human dignity, that did not cave into the lies and lusts for power and greed that was flowing and flying around so easily and willing to break the United States apart.

On January 6, 2021, the outgoing President tried to overturn the legitimate counting of the Electoral College votes that would ratify his defeat. Encouragement by him and other speakers was given to his fellow supporters, some political supporters from his Republican Party, extremist groups, some with weapons, and curious bystanders to charge to the nation's capital with force to cause upheaval in overturning the government and democracy. He further assured them that he would be there with them. He did not follow through as a few staff people held him back knowing that what he was promoting was constitutionally and dangerously wrong.

Some of the extremist groups of rioters consisted of:

Proud Boys-western chauvinists, fascists, so willing to impede the certification of Congress regarding President Biden's election to take back their country.

Oath Keepers-militia group, heavy in weapons and training for battles, stormed the capitol to stop the certification of Biden's 2020 election victory.

QAnon-Lack of respect for truth or life, twist good into evil, willing to kill. One would see deep sensitivity training here.

BLM-Black Lives Matter - Marxist in origin, looting, property damage, bloodshed, violence. Defunding the police was an outcry from their movement. Channel news. New York's mayor-elect stands up to BLM bullies, Cal Thomas, Star Advertiser, 11-16-21. 11 involved in Capitol riot accused of sedition, by Michael Balsamo, Colleen Long and Alanna Durkin Richer-Associated Press, Star Advertiser 1-14-22. Member of Proud Boys admits role in Jan. 6 riot by Michael Kunzelman and Lindsay Whitehurst-Associated Press, Star Advertiser, 12-23-21.

Others

Sadly, rioters from the negative sectors of these and other extremist groups overtook common sense and the peaceful segment of their extremist groups. For example, with BLM, many people supported them with sincerity because they believed that black lives do matter, that we all are one human race, that we are all equal, all must work to make a living, and all must be protected. But when looting and violence were seen as their aim, some BLM members who thought it was a righteous group, as well as supporters, took a step back and said, hey, wait a minute, we may be exploited by this group. Peaceful protesting was not clearly seen at all times. Other extremists with the same Marxist goals also joined in their marches. This added to the violence and looting that unfolded in some areas.

It was the Police who emerged out of duty to defend and protect law abiding citizens from unruly protestors in our States of America. In turn, these disorderly protestors lashed at our Police with rudeness, shouting profanities, using physical aggression, displaying vulgarity, and abusiveness towards them.

The defunding of the police, the very ones that face risks and fight evil on a daily basis to protect the freedom and common good for all of us, was also a strategy used to gain control and power over people through the avenue of violence. Another avenue of destroying democracy. Cases of police brutality were used to overcast the importance of all policing. Both Republicans and Democrats fell under this spell in the beginning.

Instead of defunding the police, more funding is needed to bring about accountability, and in each case with justifiable outcomes. Proper RE-training is a must when warranted, and the monitoring of police officers should be implemented with needed support. And yes, do fund other social resources besides the police to provide the necessary treatment for other ills of society.

Removing or defunding all police is comparable to the Church removing the prayer of St. Michael the Archangel from Mass to protect all, especially our souls from evil, as we face and fight daily the warfare on this earth that is shared with the fallen angels. Souls are less protected, and now if defunding the police is implemented, the lives of humans are also less protected. In 2021, one Church, after streaming the Holy Sacrifice of the Mass on TV, added on the Prayer of St. Michael the Archangel when Mass was over. There is hope, for, with faith, there is courage.

Moving on, rioters listened to the encouragement from the defeated president and speakers who further riled them up with arrogance and wrath. They all believed the propaganda emitting from him and his fellow speakers. And so, with military weapons, along with baseball bats, bear spray, hockey sticks, batons stolen from the capital police, and any other weaponry that could be used, with anger and hate they wildly attacked and stormed the nation's capital. Because such deadly force was used, a bloodbath was in the making. Among the crowd were some innocent bystanders and spectators just watching to see what it was all about.

Many capitol police and others were severely injured as the highly enraged rioters rampaged with defiance through the hallways and rooms looking and chanting to hang Vice President Pence and hunting for House Speaker Pelosi. Congress members were deliberately placed under fear, hiding in the wings to protect themselves, stopping the counting of the electoral votes for a while. While this continued on, it was reported in the news media that the president enjoyed watching all of this on TV. He allowed and saw to it that the siege is in action for a time before asking that it be stopped only through the heeding of family members or others.

Storming the United States Capitol, January 6, 2021

Presidential election, US electoral college certificates, January 6, 2021

Insurrection, January 6, 2021
Interior damage at the Nation's Capital.

Tear Gas outside of the United States Capitol, January 6, 2021, Insurrection.

Outside display while shouting to hang the Vice President inside and outside of the Nation's Capital, January 6, 2021.

Promoting aggressive violent behavior.

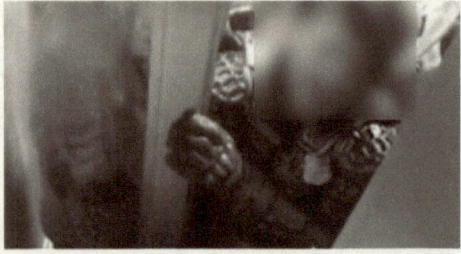

Screenshot of Capitol Police Officer being crushed during the attack on January 6, at the Insurrection on the Nation's Capital.

Pictures of the Insurrection on January 2021 are from www.google.com

Truth and courage always bring strength into focus. After being under siege for a time, Congress, in an acquiesced manner, continued its counting of the electoral votes that ratified his defeat. Because of a deliberate Marxist/ Communist plan, with lies that led to anger, hate, and then violence, five innocent lives were lost. When four police officers gave true testimony as to what happened, they were criticized by most Republicans and their favored TV news station.

This insurrection on January 6, 2021, leaves a deep negative mark in our history, showing the entire world how Americans, once seen as the highest nation in the world, can stoop so low and fall into iniquity and unprincipled, immoral, nefarious wicked behavior. It also showed how our Republican Party was no longer the strong, staunch party that upheld the values and strength of democracy and the Constitution of the United States of America. From being highly respected as a political party, it was now seen to be following a path to destroy democracy, along with its new media stations with no regard for the lives of Americans and the Constitution of the United States of America. A very high percentage of true patriots of America, of all ages, were extremely angry, disgusted, and shocked as to what took place and faced much embarrassment, ridicule, and sadness, as the entire world looked upon us.

The nation's democracy and constitution were attacked. There was a tremendous loss of moral soundness and honor that spontaneously and surprisingly, brought about a reverse, the courage to fight for our democracy.

THE AFTERMATH OF THE SIEGE AND INSURRECTION REVEALS THE LACK OF CONSTITUTIONAL INSIGHT, CLARITY, AND STANDARDS OF ETHICS

What is happening to our Republican Party, a party that was once in union with the Democrats, and together upheld the values of America?

The aftermath of this insurrection remained along the very same pathway. Lies, twisting of truths, and cover-ups or excuses continued as some members of the Republican Party, once a pivotal stronghold for democracy and highly respected, were now moving downwards towards communistic autocratic goals in smashing human dignity, human values, rights, and the destruction of democracy. It called **this insurrection as just taking a tour or a visit** through the nation's capital. Americans who witnessed it through clear vision knew it was a deceptive and cover-up statement. Moreover, in reality, many people, especially police officers suffered many injuries, including the brain, spinal, limbs, mental, and even death.

Comments tangled with warped thinking and lies were read and heard in many news media, write-ups, and newspapers throughout the nation. This great injustice reminds one of the suffering and extermination of the Jews, and others, Roma and Poles, at Auschwitz, Germany, by Hitler and his Nazi German forces in which a lie was initiated as a cover-up, denying that ever happened.

Other news sources released that some Republican congress members and individuals would also **admit that the defeated President was the key person and was morally responsible for the insurrection. Yet, they would deny such in court procedures**, that he was not responsible. Human integrity was being diminished because of fear or underlining greed for power, and perhaps the loss of jobs and rash treatments (due to opposition to do wrong) that hid behind it all.

What changed the defeated president from his very young years? He certainly was not born this way. Where did his grooming come from that warped and blinded the goodness within him, for there is goodness within but hidden. It must be nourished or it may die out. The same could be said for his political and other followers.

Over the years, many of us, including many of you, dear readers, have been told that when an organization, system, or individual commits actions that lack morals and continuously do so after being corrected by others, the key is to follow where the money is moving. The culprits will be revealed, those that have been turned into self-centered individuals and are enraptured with lust for power, and greed will be revealed. And their actions will occur over the manipulation and expense of others. There is no love of neighbor. Ultimately, no real and sincere love of God/ a higher Power.

Another example of this is when a Republican politician drew a picture of himself killing a Democratic Congresswoman with a sword and placed it on social media. The average American knows that this is certainly unacceptable, especially from a congressman. American citizens would be arrested for doing this, as **death threats** are seen there. But it was passed off by the person responsible and his supporters **that it was just a cartoon**. Lawmaker defiant as House censures him for violent post, by Kevin Freking and Brian Slodysko-Associated Press, Star Advetiser 11-18-21. Perhaps, this might be a cover-up from a sensitivity training perpetrator as well?

Suppressing Elections, and Gerrymandering/Manipulating with Electoral Mapping

Marxist/ Communistic ideologies and behaviors are so prevalent now in how the Republicans are attempting to suppress, subvert, and restrict the voting process. Republicans may be aware, some unaware, as to the subversion procedures that are flooding their party and where their former leader and party are taking them. White supremacy is showing its ugly face. In order for their party to win an election, they are limiting the number of voting places, attacking mail-in ballots by lessening them and reducing hours or days. In addition, they are even denying the second greatest commandment by God by arresting those who give water or food to citizens in need that are standing in long lines, waiting for their turn to cast their votes.

All of these negative actions are aimed at areas and states that promote the equality of diverse ethnic groups and low economic groups of people. One would say that this is overt destruction of the democratic ideals in the constitution of America, leading to fascism, racism, and atheism. I wouldn't doubt that there may be some Democrats that are also caught to some degree in several of the underhanded movements taking place in the government. No one is spared when diabolical movements are in motion.

Another area of voter suppression is in the electoral maps that are replanned every 10 years after a decennial census. Republicans are trying to gerrymander and manipulate the maps to receive more seats. And this can occur while receiving fewer votes. As a result, this can make less the votes of people of democracy, and more so, people of color. Why is this allowed? Where is Congress in also updating government to the righteousness of the reality of life?

Voting is a right for every citizen to help the government know where we should be moving to. It is not inherent in government to command what we should do.

Use of media

A few news media supported the ex-president and progressive communistic thinking by using piquant, stinging statements and any avenue of thought to change good actions into negative ones. Seeds of negativity and doubt are planted outwardly at first before any good that the person is doing is reported upon. A sly way of promoting doubt and fear in people. When faced in court for promoting such lies, these sources of the news media defended themselves by stating that it is their job to over exaggerate and stretch the news regardless if it is seen and results as lies or calumny, backbiting, or misrepresentation to viewers. In essence that is what they were hired to do. Some would say, isn't this also a type of thinking from sensitivity training? Just say what you want to, regardless if it results in a lie.

Is that how news media should function?

Misuse Of The First Amendment As A Right to Lie

Another case, an extreme one, is a man who used the first amendment, the freedom of speech, to spread a lie about the killings of the little children in a school. He publicly claimed it was a government plot and not the result of a person who went on a shooting spree. He stated that he had the right to say whatever he wanted to. Another result of sensitivity training. Does it also reflect the neglect of the Supreme Court to clarify the ethical standards and insights of the Constitution?

Then there are those who also misuse the first amendment saying it is their right not to be vaccinated due to the COVID 19 strains, knowing but not believing that they can die as well as cause the death of others. The first amendment was never meant to be used with such blindness to truths or grave possibilities that may result to themselves or others. But then, because governments in all nations have hidden truths throughout the ages, various degrees of mistrust will always be there.

Supreme Court Nomination-seething of racism

This dividedness among the two political parties in our government that is the result of Freemason/ Marxist/ Communism ideologies infiltrating particularly one party more than the other showed its ugly head by exposing in clear view to the nation to see, the lack of ethics in America, and the seething of racism in the nomination of America's first black woman of high caliber to the Supreme Court of the United States of America in March of 2022. The worst harassment, grueling, and taunting was thrown at her by members of the Republican party, very unnecessary and unwarranted in the manner chosen to do so. The constant badgering, lack of respect for her as a person in not allowing her to answer at times, and lack of respect for the process of the hearings and time allotted showed how the lust for power and greed existed within those who displayed such behaviors.

This happened before with others on the supreme court, but not to the ugly decree as was done here as verified by a congress member. Star-Advertiser, Huse and Weisman, New York Times, March 2022. It was also a very rude awakening for many young innocent voters invested with values to help our country. Where are the ethical standards for conducting such hearings?

And again, within the Supreme Court, where are the ethical standards when a spouse of a judge is caught in a situation to destroy the nation's democracy? This also came out in the news and media in March of 2022.

Supreme Court - Roe versus Wade – Constitutional Amendments- lack of clarity and insight

Along with attempting to control elections and the nation's Supreme Court functions and nominations, (so politically benched and was planned to be so by the former president for his ends in mind and not that of the people), in May of 2022, underlying currents were trying to control the inalienable right of a woman, by denying the right of every woman their freedom of choice to make their own personal decision regarding their body. This choice belongs to those personally involved, and ultimately that of the woman and her higher power. This lust for control from those with freemason/ Marxist/ communistic goals in mind, knowingly or unknowingly, or politically influenced, will lead to further abuse of Americans.

Comparable to this is, as mentioned earlier when the church decided that at childbirth when both lives are in danger, the mother and the unborn, the mother should die. Life is from God and should come about through personal commitment with God, especially through Holy Matrimony. This decision belongs only to those personally involved. It is their inalienable right, purely personal, and does not belong to the government or church to decide.

The freedom of choice for Men and Women should be respected when it concerns areas of other personal and mutual choices such as the use of birth control in marriages due to circumstances.

Included also is the gender preference opposite of the biological gender if it is naturally instilled during the embryonic developmental stages of a human being due to Mother Nature falling asleep during this crucial time or due to other social upbringings. With sanctifying grace given to the soul and with the workings of the Holy Spirit, the pull of the soul towards God awakens and the biological gender takes its rightful place. This may take years later in life, or sooner, or not at all. It is between God and a soul. When it is begotten from a natural state of life and is of innocence, we need to support it even if we do not comprehend it.

The misuse of such personal inalienable rights that results in abuse of the physical, mental, emotional, and spiritual aspects of a person, such as the violation of human rights with coerced and even willing male and female prostitutes, sex trafficking, and the like, is where mandated laws and rules have a definitive role to play. However, they should be determined with input from those who are medical or social experts in the prevention of such crimes.

Moreover, laws and rules that apply to females and males should always include both female and male qualified input. There is a tremendous lack of understanding when males draw up laws or rules for females and vice versa when females create laws for males. Common sense should prevail.

Personal Political Relationships Resulting In Financial Gains Prevents Justice

Most importantly, these behaviors reveal outwardly the lack of values, lack of human dignity, and respect in America. This is coupled with the news from many media sources including magazines, about the financial gains of the children of the presidents of both parties that were received from foreign countries. It revealed the **lack of ethics** also in this area of huge financial deals that can affect military relations as in Syria, relations with China, and criminal accountability in Saudi Arabia.

The nation waited to see what the former president was going to do to bring Saudi Arabia to justice for the deliberate killing of the American journalist, Jamal Khashoggi. Nothing was done, probably due to a tremendous financial deal made with his family member, and other ties with Saudi Arabia. This grows into an alliance with Arabia for a promotion support should he run for office again. Article by Timothy O'Brien, Star-Advertiser. This was also seen on the TV news media. This chicanery results in much fraud due to its deceptive elements.

LACK OF STANDARDS AND ETHICS KILLS JUSTICE THROUGHOUT THE NATION OF AMERICA

Congress, Supreme Courts, Military Courts, Prosecuting Attorney Offices, Etc.

By May of 2022, many Americans viewed the Supreme Court as being too political in how they functioned, more by their political ties and beliefs rather than guided by the nation's law. Because of its draft opinion to overturn Roe vs. Wade, resulting from a political move, a person remarked on leaving the country and moving to another country that respects the freedom of choice.

Moreover, some perceived that without term limits on the Supreme Court, they are losing touch with the real America and the real issues of Americans. Hubler and Wines, New York Times, May 5, 2022. This is certainly true if the Supreme Court is at odds with one another due to politics and supremacist attitudes.

Then there are some of the judges that declare their stand on issues that affect American citizens, and once appointed to the Supreme Court, take an entirely different stand contrary to what they had promised.

Racism and white supremacy that promotes hate, appear to be negatively leading to some decisions that affect all citizens. Truths must come to the foreground. Slavery must be studied so that it does not happen again. All races must be respected and dignified as belonging to the human race. There is no room for the Great Replacement Theory, pushed by the media, that suggest the white race is being overshadowed by other races. Rather, itself is trying to overshadow other races due to its lust for power and greed. Star-advertiser, 5-18-22, Tony Norman, Pittsburg Post-Gazette. And in reality, it is being joined together with all races' inequality and readily accepted by many of its ethnic members.

Some states of America are ahead of the federal government. Standards of Ethics are implemented on the state level in its functioning whether in relations or finances and other areas, in order to prevent discrimination, racism, favoritism, I scratch your back- you scratch mine, favors, bribery, lies, controlling through politics, and the like, all that leads to lawlessness and favoring of the perpetrator. If negligence occurs due to a lack of monitoring, the very areas under protection will be severely violated. The judicial department must deal with its consequences if these violations do occur, which may include fines, incarceration, or both along with jail time. Resignations, suspensions, and dismissals should result from top officials and others who are in charge if there is deliberate neglect. If not, the will of the people will not be addressed, nor will democracy. Justice then plunges off the cliff.

Evil within the Government to go ahead   vs   Evil within the Church and the need for correction

FEBRUARY 20, 2022 a news article stated the following: "Open your eyes, many in our government worship satan, that was published in 2017 on an online message. News article by David Kirkpatrick, New York Times. This time period coincided with the formation of extremist groups. Evidently, this message is alleged to have been written by an extremist, which in turn sparked many other extremists to move towards negative activities and behaviors, thinking they would be supported by government satanic worshippers with freemason/ Marxist/ communist ideologies. And in a sense, they were correct as this was and is seen as time marches on, with the lies, the insurrection on January 6, 2021, and warping of truths, twisted behaviors, and messages taking place among some congressmen and women and their followers of the right-wing party.

Would not Christians want their churches to speak out on these issues in their homilies? In support of God, not a political party. That is a separation of church and state.

Following post-Vatican II, in 1967, Pope Paul VI remarked, "By some fissure, there has entered into the temple of God the smoke of satan: there is doubt, uncertainty, problems, unrest." By 2022, many attempts to correct and fight the smoke have been undertaken by the Popes, bishops, priests, and the church with success amid many upheavals, confusions, and contentions that are still ongoing. The people are speaking out and some officials are finally listening.

In a sense, the majority of the democratic party is fighting against the evil within the government fueled by some of the members of the right-wing party that had readily spread like COVID. People are also speaking truths, but not all are listening and being blinded by lies. With God, the blinders will be removed.

AMERICA NEEDS TO BE AWAKEN

This lack of choice to choose good on the national scale is fulfilling all of the steps of Freemasons and Marxists Communism that swiftly went into high gear years before but more so after the Cold War (1947-1991 with the dissolution of the Soviet Union) to destroy democracy, and take over a nation as an autocratic regime. Right now**, it appears that the dissolution of the Soviet Union was only a front** to cover up its continual goal to conquer all nations to exist as communist countries, and ultimately as a communist world government, especially those countries that were once a part of Russia in the past. So does China, another communist country, have this also in mind with Taiwan? What about the other communist countries that control peoples' lives, their thinking with heavy propaganda, covering truths all for the lust of power and greed, such as North Korea, and perhaps Viet Nam?

If both parties, Democrats, and Republicans, do not awaken to work together, communism will become stronger and both parties will dissipate into vapors leaving the way for communistic autocratic authoritarianism world government to take control. Result: the new world where absolutely no freedom will exist for any of its citizens. No one will have the right to choose good. Is this not a goal of the fallen angels as well? The life of a human being will not be of any use to the autocrats.

THE ATTACK ON UKRAINE BY RUSSIA

This movement towards a communistic autocratic dictatorship, a fascist world government that oppresses with violence anyone with different viewpoints, is seen as Russia's leader and military forced and bullied its way surrounding **Ukraine**, a peaceful nation in its own right on **February 24, 2022.** Because **the annihilation** of Ukraine could not occur **from within** due to the Faith of its people, Russia resorted to annihilating **from without,** with physical warfare, military weaponry, killings, and bombings under another big lie. Besides using the fact that because it was once part of Russia as an underlying reason for its attack, Russia is emphasizing that it needs to rid Ukraine of Nazi leaders and Nazi sympathizers. This is so contrary to the truth as Ukraine's leader and others are Jews. The Philadelphia Inquirer. Many innocent people, men, women, and children have suffered and died as a result of Russia's deliberate assault on the cities, homes, schools, hospitals, and churches in Ukraine. And the ex-president of America praised Putin for attacking Ukraine, calling him a smart person, a genius.

As time went on, the courageous Ukrainians led by their president of great integrity, Volodymyr Zelensky, continued to fight back. In addition, while NATO and others sanctioned Russia, the ex-president of the United States started to change his tune, a behavior that is seen whenever it benefits himself and his cult and not surprisingly so. This is ironic as the ex-president appeared to be close to Putin in order to be an authoritarian leader like him. Unknowingly should he achieve such, it could happen that he ends up being a puppet in his mentor's hands.

Moreover, if this type of world government should occur, the lust for power and greed, and other capital sins may result in more wars for just one person to be the supreme president of the entire world. War is the result of evil. Other dictators will be puppets to this world government president.

Putin's attack on Ukraine is comparable to the Papacy forming the first Crusade in 1095 to brutally strike peaceful Muslim villages, leaving many suffering in the aftermath. The reason was to help others and capture the Holy Land, Jerusalem. A holy and religious reason is a common camouflage to hide behind hidden goals related somewhat to the seven capital sins. Other crusades followed with additional goals in the making. And both sides, the Arabs and the Christians/Catholics had their hidden agendas such as richness, along with the suffering of people, cannibalism, boiling and eating of humans, staking children, exploiting the innocence, the raping and violence of women and men, the destruction of villages, and the coveting of their food, water, homes. A friend by the name of Joe L. shared a very interesting book with me. One should read about the two sides of the crusades, that of the Christians and that of the Muslims such as "The Crusades Through Arab Eyes by Amon Maalouf."

The crimes of warfare with the Crusades and Arabs are equivalent to what all are witnessing that is happening to Ukraine by the attacks of the Russian military. So many carnages are occurring with the bombing of structures where people live, besides buildings of businesses, health, learnings, and all other aspects that sustain life. These are resulting in the deaths of many including citizens, innocent men, women, children, and even animals. Many Ukrainians sheltered themselves in basements or subways lacking food, water, medicine, toiletries, and the necessities for life. Violence, beatings on the human body along with removing all fingernails, the shoving of items into the oral openings of the body, extreme suffering, the bonding of hands with tape or ropes, killings even on sight, killings after raping, some violations even performed in front of parents and children, all sounds so familiar.

Star-Advertiser 4-4-22, P. A7, Carlotta Gail, Andrew R. Kramer, and Ivor Prickett, New York Times.

> scape of mangled tank hulks, snapped trees and rattled but resilient survivors.
>
> There are also stories, impossible to verify, highlighting the kind of hate left in an occupation's wake and sharing a common thread of brutality: children held at knifepoint; an old woman forced to drink alcohol as her occupiers watched and laughed; whispers of rape and forced disappearances; and an old man found toothless, beaten in a ditch and defecated on.
>
> "Oh, God, how I wanted to
>
> exploded shells, grenade and other scattered expl sives. Other men cannit ized destroyed Russian armored vehicles for p working machinery.
>
> "I can't wrap my h around how this wa tanks and missiles i ble," said Olena Vol the head doctor at t tal and the deputy the town council. " who? The peaceful "This is true bar she said.
>
> THE WAR BEGA

Star-Advertiser 4-4-22, P. A3, Thomas Gibbins-Neff and Natalia Yermak, New York Times.

Such **barbaric atrocities** committed by the Russians still occurring in 2022! In addition, to further destroy all life in Ukraine, bombs, booby traps, and explosives are secretly hidden in areas where citizens would most likely return to, their homes, cars, washing machines, even loved ones, under corpses, on medical gurneys, and the like.

War is evil. Some will say that sometimes, war is a necessary evil, to protect what is good. Is it really? Look at our failures in Vietnam, in Afghanistan. Instead of just fighting to protect something of goodness, satanic acts come into play. So many civilian lives of all ages are lost along with human atrocities. I remember reading a news article long ago about a soldier who admitted that during wartime, he had raped a young civilian girl, and then killed her. He said that he did not know what overcame him, and just did it as if out of control, as some others were doing it also. The essential question is: to whom did you turn over the control of your soul and body if you do not know what overcame you?

The suffering and killing of innocent children, the raping and violence along with the killings of women and men by attackers, all are in the violation of the human soul and body and are utter violations of humans on this earth and **extreme diabolical actions.** Fair justice and fair courts without racist attitudes must deal with these human violations on earth. And ultimately, all souls belong to God. We must all answer to God for our actions.

Because all souls belong to God, we are given the freedom of choice. This connection to goodness is seen in many Russians who bravely protest the attack on Ukraine from their own government, to **destroy from without**. Their protest of fortitude was seen or heard in many different ways, in posts on supermarket shelves, in signs, in sermons at churches, and on networks. Because of their outward courage in fighting against the large scale of propaganda that is used by Russia to blind its own Russian citizens to the truth of their attack to annihilate Ukraine, these people of faith, of goodness, are arrested, charged with a fine, or tortured. Each of us is responsible for our actions, good or bad. Or gray.

Police officers prepare to detain Dmitry Reznikov near the Kremlin in Moscow as he holds a piece of paper with asterisks on it that could have been interpreted as "No to war" in Russian. He was fined $618 for the brief demonstration.

Russian speaking out against the war in Ukraine.
Star-Advertiser, Friday, 4/15/22 p. A10

Our Lady of Fatima stated that many souls will be martyred.

In the hell of this war, the Ukrainians held on to their faith in God/their Higher Power, to values, maintained a sanguine spirit with one another, fought the warfare with fortitude, courage, and their lives in preserving their faith and the right to choose to live in a Democratic Nation.

Prayer and penance are needed. Russia needs to be consecrated to Her Immaculate Heart.

A BRIEF REVIEW OF GOALS THAT CAN DESTROY OR ANNIHILATE A NATION:

Freemasons: planned and written (Alta Vendita) over a hundred years ago:

-The **subversion of the Catholic Church,** to destroy and infiltrate it under the disguises of modernism(subjectivity), liberalism(ambiguity), and progressivism (humanism embedded in radical liberalism), yet appearing so Apostolic in order to carry out and further its hidden agenda.

-Move beliefs regarding the doctrines and the teachings of Christ of the religious and lay people, from under the disguise of the spiritual to humanism, yet having them believe that they are still faithful and staunch Catholics.

-Groom and infiltrate the training of the upcoming priests, bishops, and cardinals in these areas so that a pope will emerge from them that will promote progressivism to the fullest.

-The terms such as enlightenment, renewal, and ecumenical would be used as a cover-up.

Marxist Communism:

-People were no longer allowed to worship God or even conduct religious services, the movement toward atheism and religious indifference.

-Any denial of a state order was met with fear, being arrested, interred, and tortured, and executing one's freedom of the will was met with violence.

-Total authoritarianism was promoted and in essence, freedom of the will to choose good given by God Almighty was removed from all human citizens. Evil was coerced to overpower good.

-Traditions from the past were annihilated.

-Ownership by the government capital and products, no one could own private property, an element of humanistic socialism.

-Marriage was just considered a public registry, its sanctity and vows in Holy Matrimony being extinguished.

-Crusade Magazine, P.O. Box 341, Hanover, PA 17331 September/October 2017 p.12.

COMMUNISM A book titled The Naked Communist, states the communist goals along with the promotion of Marxism: FC 123 p.22, 2018

-Break down morality with the promotion of pornography, books, magazines, motion pictures, TV, and radio.

-Destroy families by promoting promiscuity, masturbation, and divorce.

-Break up the safe world of children, raise them away from parental influence.

-Change the outlook of homosexuality, degeneracy, and promiscuity as normal, natural, and healthy.

-Use infiltration to destroy the catholic church, its leaders, clergy, and the faith of its people under destructive auspices that would appear to be holy and religious.

All of the goals have and are continuing to be met up to the present time. What stand will the United States of America take? To remain united or be divided.

WHAT CAN BE DONE TO COUNTERACT THESE NEGATIVE AND DIABOLICAL GOALS?

So much can be done to save the United States of America from being annihilated as a nation of the highest standing in the world where one can live in peace. Am sure that you, Reader, have some suggestions. Here are just a few options:

CONTINUE TO HOLD AMERICA STRONG?

Values -Family, Children, Education, Society

The basic values of life, integrity, honesty, respect, truthfulness, political and social equality, and others that lead to a decent and peaceful life under a government FOR and BY the people, need to be re-installed in every individual, in our families, and in our society.

It should promote every individual to hold on to Truth, and the Freedom of the Will to choose good. The individual can then grow in piety and feel his/her soul reaching to a level beyond the intellect, towards a spiritual existence of extreme Goodness.

These elements are important especially when we fall into sin under the weight of our crosses in life, so that we can get up and continue to carry our crosses moving forward to God.

Husbands and wives will be supported to live out their vows in Holy Matrimony and marriage and if God is willing, provide a safe and loving home for their children.

It is everyone, including the single person as well the youth and children that live out the inherent positive values at birth that is nourished by others through periods of growth. They stand for what is right for themselves and others, respecting the dignity of humans, the right to choose good, the fortitude to speak the truth and fight for it, and the strength to stand up for God when they fall under their crosses. They have no fear because they know that fear is from evil, and that the father of all lies is the devil.

It is also and so very important and crucial to remember the lives of millions of our military Veterans in every branch, Army, Navy, Marines, and Air Force, who fought with dedication and bravery and who gave up their lives, just so each one of us, from every ethnic background, can live freely in America. They enlisted or were drafted to fight for our freedom to be able to freely choose, whether to walk in the parks, visit families, take in movies, go to schools of choice, elect our government officials on the state and federal levels, or perhaps to include Supreme Court members, and live a life of choice. We need to uphold and protect their memories, that their service, their sufferings, and perhaps of abuse also, that their sacrifice for our country was not in vain; that in union with their efforts and lives, we, too, stand that our DEMOCRATIC government of the United States of America exists FOR and BY the People.

What other sources are there to promote this great change of growth?

Government

The American citizenry must call to task all political leaders to be upright in their responsibilities in protecting the democracy of the United States of America, especially those who undermine the rights of Americans due to corporates or others that put money into their pockets with their lust for power. VOTE!

Congress must protect the Constitution of the United States of America, its democracy, its rightful laws, and the freedom and right of every American citizen to vote freely and live in peace. The freedom and right to vote by every single American Citizen is the strength of a democracy and must be preserved at all times.

No president, member of Congress, member of the Supreme Court, judges and courts, and the Military should be given any power to act as a puppet or leader to promote Freemason/ Marxist/ Communist ideologies that heavily influenced other government leaders like Hitler of Germany, and Lenin of Russia and other isotope followers around the world including America, to dominate with fear, lies, and suppression in controlling the intellectual thinking, the lives, and imposed immoral choices upon its citizenry. There is no room for lies, fear, and racism/ supremacy that promotes hate that leads to violence.

Democrats and Republicans, if the two-party system is to continue to exist, must work together in all honesty and truthfulness for the sake of the people, and put aside personal agendas. There is no room in a democratic government for the lust for power, control, suppression of opposition, greed, hate, racism, white supremacy, fear, and lies. These elements of capital sins are not to be tolerated as they lead to total destruction. Silent Republicans and others need to overcome their fears of being coerced or threatened by their colleagues, and their so-called groomers should justly be reprimanded, regardless of their present or previous status, and remember as to why they are serving as government officials- to protect democracy, FOR and BY the people.

This came out strongly with the shooting of 19 students and two teachers at another Elementary School in Texas. Why are you in your political positions in Congress was asked of the Senate, as they refrain from doing what needs to be done if it affects their lust for power and money?

The Republican Party and the Democratic Party must maintain their positions with decency, truthfulness, moral and human integrity, honesty, respect for diversity, working together in shared resolutions, and protecting our human rights, and our democracy. Freemason/ Marxist /communist thinking Republicans, and should there be Democrats and others in the citizenry, need to leave and release their lives of hate, bigotry, racial supremacy, fascist's attitudes, and change to return to our goals of democracy. If they refuse to do so and are not interested in protecting democracy, then they are free to resign from their offices and relocate to other communist countries where they would be happy with their lust for autocratic power and money. Freedom of choice.

Church-Spirit of Humans

Because some of the outcomes of Vatican II resulted in placing Humanity as the center of life, Churches need to bring God back as the center of human life to guide humanity, by uplifting the spirit, the soul, towards heavenly graces, the love of God, and the love of neighbor. The spirit must lead the soul in relation to its human body and its needs in The Reality of Life on Earth by God Almighty. This is seen by many Christians.

Due to the arrows purposely thrown from the freemason/ Marxist/ communists to push the church downward in order to destroy it, the faithful, the laity, and believers must support the church and call it to the task of returning to its purpose on earth, not to impose unacceptable changes that separate a soul from God's love or neglect to do the necessary changes needed to unite souls to God in the Reality of Life on Earth.

A Vatican III Council is just a thought, to update, for example, **living the Ten Commandments to the Life of Reality while remaining connected to God**, not by negating them and shoving them into the shadows of the background. Situation Ethics, if done rightfully, and with clarity, can help tremendously in this area.

It is important that churches reflect inwardly and bring about the changes that would develop good solid values based on the teachings of Jesus Christ that people can follow in this Life of Realty. This will enhance the spiritual lives and FAITH of their parishioners. This review should include correcting writing errors, especially those that have existed since the inception of the books of the Bible, by separating Biblical cultural aspects that oppose the teachings of Christ, and correcting or updating cultural terminology in the Bible that would be in alignment with the teachings of Jesus.

A perfect example of this is found in the new Catechism of the Catholic Church. Long ago, as stated earlier, it was taught that all souls that commit suicide are condemned to hell. Many regular parishioners wondered about this. There are souls that sincerely cry out for help from the depths of their hearts and souls, while on earth, and no help is given. Suicide is committed. Certainly, they are not deserving of hell.

Finally, after many years, the new Catechism, now reflects the change that was needed, that these souls are no longer condemned. Others may be. Only God knows. But now, how does the church make up for this mistake? As with sending mothers to their graves? Food for deep thought. What can the faithful also do to heal this area?

"Whatever you shall bind on earth shall be bound in heaven, and whatever you shall lose on earth shall be loosed in heaven." Matthew 16:19 Some ministers have used this statement from Jesus and applied it to the forgiveness of sins, such as, whatever sins you forgive are forgiven, whatever sins you retain are retained. Sins retained then must be dealt with justice in mind, provided the Justice department on earth is based on fair ethical standards and not politics, racism, discrimination, or hatred. Sometimes, God uses and allows earthly forces besides spiritual or even both to deal with sinners, such as imprisonment, and capital punishment.

The church can help in reviewing the role of the Mother of God in overseeing the entire church and the role of Her Son, Jesus Christ, in being the essence of the church. This can be paralleled to how nuns can oversee the entire church as Mary Immaculate, and how priests are to protect the essence of the church with Jesus in the sacraments, preaching, rituals, etc., and add strength to its functioning. Both are equal in God's eyes.

Therefore, it is crucial that the pope, cardinals, bishops, priests, religions, and nuns fulfill their vows such as in Holy Orders, as well as ministers in other denominations, in following the footsteps of Jesus Christ Who Has Come in the Flesh, with purity, poverty, and obedience, teaching what He gave to us while on this earth.

Its leaders, who need our prayers as we also need theirs, should exemplify the life of Christ along with all of us as believers, as we fight this earthly warfare along with all of us in the midst of the vapors of the 7 capital sins. Preaching the words of Christ should enable Christians to choose what God asks of us. If a choice is made in contrast but with deep faith, then the decision between the Christian and God should be supported with prayer, mercy, and understanding with God as the final judge.

Changes need to be explained with a clear understanding as much as possible so they do not lead to confusion and excessive and abusive usage such as in situation ethics and the new Catechism for Catholics, which was done well but some clarity is still needed. With patience and enlightenment, insights will occur in God's time.

Moreover, and very importantly, the training of seminarians should result in the service to God and not of man or communistic ideas or goals. The disciplines of Philosophy and Theology should be revisited in their training, in communion with the teachings of Jesus Christ and not teachings by professors that deny the Trinity and Divinity of Jesus. In one instance, when such a professor who denied the Trinity and Divinity of Jesus was asked to resign, and not be fired, the counteraction was stated as an infraction of academic freedom. How ludicrous can humans be! Lies are not deserving of any academic freedoms! FC Issue 122 Summer 2018. Archbishop Fulton Sheen, as a visionary, besides many other devout Christians, also sees that moving and conquering mass upheavals is through the spirit in all segments of each person's life.

Regarding celibacy in the priesthood or religious life, as a devoted priest, Father Stephen T. once shared succinctly with me, that the energies of sex are transformed onto the spiritual level to minister to souls moving them forward to the spiritual plane towards God. This flows along with the vows of Poverty, Chastity, and Obedience. With all of the free sex that has occurred among some religious, the concept of marriage is thought of vs. celibacy. Perhaps, these can then serve as deacons. Those whose commitment is to celibacy, as that of Father Stephen, can then be fully commissioned to carry out the function of Holy Orders and with Our Heavenly Father, transform the bread and the wine into the Body and Blood of Jesus Christ in the sacrament of Holy Eucharist. Just a thought.

WHAT IS THE STRONGEST POWER TO COUNTERACT THE EVIL THAT AMERICA AND THE WORLD FACE?

MOTHER OF GOD - FATIMA

For **Everyone**, Catholics, non-Catholics, mystics, visionaries, believers, and non-believers, Heaven sent us a pathway to have Peace on Earth through prayer and penance.

The plan from heaven, the request from the Mother of God, Mary Immaculate when She appeared at Fatima, that the Pope with all the catholic bishops in the world in community with their congregations, on the same day and time, consecrates Russia to Her Immaculate Heart.

History:

The Mother of Jesus Christ appeared 6 times from May to October 1917, in the hills near Fatima, Portugal, to three children, Lucia, Jacinta, and Francisco. Her message or secret contained the following:

> To be revealed in 1927-

1. The three children were given a vision of hell that was frightening. But our Holy Mother asked for penance and prayers, especially of the Rosary for those souls in hell that wanted to be saved. Most souls are there due to sins of the flesh and indecent fashions. Find more information in Part II of this book.

2. Prediction of World War I and the beginning of World War II. The rise and fall of the Soviet Union. Request for the Communion of Reparation on the First Saturdays and that Russia be consecrated to the Immaculate Heart of Mary.

3. To be revealed in 1960 to the whole world- the tremendous upheaval within the Catholic Church; an angel with a flaming sword appears, and a person dressed in white, a bishop or man falls to the ground under a hail of gunfire; that Portugal would preserve the dogma of faith. The actual words of Our Holy Mother have not yet been released by Vatican officials as perhaps other information or revelations.

On October 13, 1917, after identifying herself as Our Lady of the Rosary, the great Miracle of the Sun was shown to an estimated 70,000 people present, many who doubted the heavenly occurrences, some just to be obstinate towards the three children and make fun of them and the entire event. Drenched with rain water, they stood in amazement and awe as the SUN, after dancing in the sky, plunged to earth, emitted multicolored lights, and then returned to its place in the sky. Immediately after its occurrence, all their wet soaked clothes were dry. And the doubters admitted their beliefs.

Picture of people witnessing the Miracle of the Sun at Fatima. (www.google.com)

Picture of the statue of Our Lady of Fatima and Our Mother of God and the three children on the wall. (www.google.com)

CONSECRATING RUSSIA

At this time, we should be seriously concerned with Russia. Regarding the consecration of Russia:

The Mother of Jesus stated clearly that Peace on Earth will be attained in the world only when Russia is consecrated to The Immaculate Heart of Mary. This consecration must be followed according to the directions given to Lucia.

1. Only Russia is to be specifically named to be consecrated (to set aside for a holy purpose.)

2. by the Pope in union with all the Catholic Bishops in the entire world, who must organize in his own diocese a public and solemn ceremony of reparation and Consecration of Russia on one special day and time (together.)

3. This conversion will be to the one true Church of Christ, the Catholic Church.

HAS ANYONE MADE THE CONSECRATION OF RUSSIA TO THE IMMACULATE HEART OF MARY?

A brief history of the sincere and brave attempts made by some of the Popes while under scrutiny and bashing from others, even their own, or may unknowingly lack the necessary information that was deliberately held back and hidden from them:

Pope Pius XI, elected pope in 1922, condemned communism.

Pope Pius XII, 1942 consecrated the world, and not Russia by name. In 1952 following a request again by the Mother of God in May, in July he consecrated Russia by name only in an Apostolic Letter, not in union with all the bishops in the world or publicly. It appears that perhaps not all information was given to him in a timely manner.

Pope John XXIII 1959 refused to release to the world in 1960 the third secret of Fatima as requested by Our Holy Mother, which included the warning that apostasy may be from the Church itself. That decay of the church may come from within it and not from the outside. Lucia was then forbidden in 1960 by Pope John XXIII to speak about the Fatima apparitions. Vatican approval had to be obtained in order to speak to her.

Vatican II then began. It resulted in the movement of placing humankind as the center of religion, and not God, and liberal progressivism captured the Council. Russian Orthodox attended with the agreement that the Papacy did not condemn communism. Unfortunately, this was in opposition to many Bishops who were not heard nor given the clarity of what was agreed upon or as to why. Other reasons may or may not have existed. However, the decision helped to dissolve a worldwide crisis.

Pope Paul VI, 1967 linked the Apocalypse, Chapter 12 to the Message of Fatima. He was deeply concerned about the gravity of changes due to Vatican II that would move the church and its teachings towards worldly goals, affecting them mentally and theologically aspects of all. Five years later he stated: "By some fissure, there has entered into the temple of God the smoke of satan: there is doubt, uncertainty, problems, unrest."

Pope John Paul I, Pope for 33 days, May 13, 1982, consecrated the world; bishops did not organize their own diocese as requested to have a public and solemn ceremony of reparation and consecration of Russia.

Pope John Paul II, March 25, 1984, consecrated the world; bishops did not organize their own diocese as requested. There were signs of bishops showing disapproval of such or saw no urgency in fulfilling the request of the Mother of God. Pope John Paul II also linked the Message of Fatima to the Apocalypse, as Pope Paul VI did. He also included the Feast of Our Lady of Fatima on May 13 in the Roman Missal. The pedophile scandal amongst others in the priesthood came to the foreground during this time.

In 2000, John Paul II finally released some of the third portions of the secret that should have been given entirely to the world in 1960 as requested, the angle with the flaming sword and a martyred pope. However, the message, the actual words, and the explanations of Our Lady were not disclosed.

Pope Benedict, on May 13, 2010, stated the Fatima event was authentic. Initiated the process by asking permission of the Russian Orthodox Patriarch, but no consecration resulted, most certainly for good and various reasons. FC issue 114. Spring 2016.

Pope Francis referred himself to be the bishop dressed in white, as contained in the third portion of the Secret of Fatima. Is he also the one as predicted by St. Malachy the prophet, to be the last Pope during this time of the persecution of the Church? Difficult to conclude as there are two Popes at this time in the Vatican. The Prophecies of St. Malachy, Peter Bander, Tan Books and Publisher, Rockford, Ill. 1973, pg.96

At a Synod under the Papacy of Pope Francis, Situation Ethics decisions regarding the 6th and 9th commandments were made in opposition to the Church's teaching under Pope John Paul II and Pope Benedict XVI. Clarity was lacking. No consecration of Russia to the Immaculate Heart was made at this time.

The Fatima Center, The Third Secret made simple. Email: info@fatima.org.com

March 25, 2022, An Act of Consecration to the Immaculate, Heart of Mary was made at the Basilica of Saint Peter, "Therefore, Mother of God and our Mother, to your Immaculate Heart we solemnly entrust and consecrate ourselves, the Church, and all humanity, especially Russia and Ukraine."

Question: Were the steps followed as stated by Our Lady of Fatima? Were all the steps finally given to the Pope to follow or is its entirety still being held back by Vatican Officials or others?

WHAT OBSTRUCTED THE PROPER PROCESS OF RUSSIA'S CONSECRATION TO THE IMMACULATE HEART OF MARY?

Research as to why this never occurred properly resulted in the following:

1. Even though most of the popes sincerely wanted to fulfill their ministry on earth and address the request of the Mother of God, not all bishops were willing or eager to move ahead in doing so. Some were progressive liberalists, while others lacked the necessary

information and the actual wordings of Our Lady that would give them the insight into seeing its importance. And then there were those who without any doubt or hesitation, wanted to fulfill their service on earth to God. The Fatima Center, The True Story of Fatima, Email: info@fatima.org.com

2. There appeared to be a deliberate and forceful holding back of information, such as the actual words or explanations among other things given by the Mother of God that was relayed to the three children. This suppressing or subversion was by adults in charge, most probably Vatican officials. To this day, so much is still concealed, placing those who are able to move forward in precarious situations. This results in holding all believers as hostages by such leaders in power, some even over-stepping the Pope or maybe previous Popes.

3. From the time they were youngsters, the three children were met with threats of death, and imprisonment, along with repulsive and abusive behaviors from others. People that attacked them came from all avenues of life. Some came from an element of masons, people who were atheists, priests, and other Christians who doubted, and people who were jealous. Because Lucia outlived her cousins, Jacinta and Francisco, she held all information dear to her heart. She never doubted even when **forbidden** by Pope John XXIII to stop speaking of it entirely, suppressing it, "as well as the diabolical disorientation among the upper hierarchy of the Church." The Fatima Center, The Third Secret Made Simple, Email: info@fatima.org.com

4. 1963 Pope Paul VI, knowingly or unknowingly, reinforced liberal progressivism by naming 3 liberal Cardinals into powerful positions out of four.

5. In 1989-1990, five false letters attributed to Lucia were written by clergy affirming that Pope John Paul II has Consecrated Russia on March 25, 1984. FC Issue 125, Winter 2019.

6. In 2000, the third part or secret, or portion of it, was forcefully revealed to the public through the efforts of a priest. Father Nicholas Gruner, who suffered much, being attacked and bashed

by another clergy over years, devoted the commitment of his vows in Holy Orders to the spread of the message of Our Lady of Fatima. He shared tremendous knowledge and love of God and the Holy Mother through his writings, preaching, and sermons, which much are shared at the Fatima Center. Because of his sharing of truths, he was crucified and demeaned by his own colleagues, a few Vatican officials, and others. This sharing of the third secret of Fatima with the public was requested to be done in 1960 by the Mother of God. Only through his endless efforts was it shared in 2000, but we are unaware if it contained all that the Mother of God stated.

7. A church cardinal stated that the third secret of the Fatima message already occurred in the 20th century and was part of the past. This was in total contrast to what Lucia was stating. The truth about it was revealed later, that it was still to be carried out as requested. FC Issue 125, Winter 2019, p. 37.

8. Regarding Marian apparitions, the Roman Catholic Church does not mandate its members to believe such claims. It is not part of any core doctrine, referred to as Deposit of Faith. www.google.com Yet, many believers know, including religious, of the sacredness of Marian apparitions, and how to decipher such, especially among visionaries.

With much-hidden manipulation and interferences, Fatima's information has been thrust into confusion leaving many believers ruminating over where its status was and is at, and of course, there are some labeling it as spurious and deceptive in all aspects. The elucidating of Fatima's message with full clarity and transparency is needed to see what Our Lady of Fatima revealed, specified, and requested. The writings of Lucia should be released in all their entirety to those clergy and believers, whether they are Catholics, Christians, or even non-Christians, who have God and Goodness as the center of their life so that the truths can be seen with clarity and accounted for, the true message and the consecration of Russia to be carried out as requested by the Mother of Jesus Christ.

WHAT WARNINGS DID THE MOTHER OF GOD GIVE TO ALL OF US IF HER REQUEST THAT RUSSIA BE CONSECRATED TO HER IMMACULATE HEART IS NOT HEEDED?

"If Russia is not consecrated, it will spread her errors throughout the world promoting wars and persecution of the Church. The good will be martyred, the Holy Father will have much to suffer and many nations will be annihilated. Finally, my Immaculate Heart will triumph. The Holy Father will consecrate Russia to me and she will be converted (Catholicism) and the world will be given a certain period of peace.

In Portugal, the dogma of the Faith will always be preserved."

The Fatima Center, The Third Secret made simple. Email: info@fatima.org.com

HOW DO WE STOP THE ANNIHILATION OF THE UNITED STATES OF AMERICA AND ITS DEMOCRACY?

Besides what was stated earlier about improving with the return of values in our lives, society, government, and church, we need to offer **Prayers and Penance, especially saying the Rosary and Communion on the First Saturdays.** Pray for those who can bring it about. Pray for the Pope, the Bishops, the Priests, ministers, religions, our government and all of America, and all of humankind, including our families and selves.

It is now up to each one of us to also take the lead and **use the gift given to us from above: THE FREEDOM OF THE WILL TO CHOOSE GOOD.**

REMEMBER, DEAR READER,

"We have a wrestling, not against blood and flesh, but against the governments, against the authorities, against the world rulers of this darkness, against the wicked spirit forces in the heavenly places."
EPHESIANS 6:12

IN THE NAME OF JESUS CHRIST WHO HAS COME IN THE FLESH, LET US ALL WORK TOGETHER WITH GOD ALMIGHTY AND PUT A STOP TO THIS DIABOLICAL DESTRUCTION. LET THERE BE PEACE ON EARTH

PEACE BE UNTO YOU.

O Mary, conceived without sin, pray for us who have recourse to you.

PART II

PROLOGUE

A WALK-THROUGH HEAVEN, EARTH, AND HELL

Why was this portion of the book written?

Its inception also dates back to the 1970s. The following portion of this book would be of interest to readers who enjoy reading about spiritual happenings or have had spiritual experiences and even further, and most importantly, who may be seeking some form of guidance. A reader may have learnt to handle them on their own, or learnt from others. In any case, those who have learnt how to handle such, by the graces of God Almighty, may I encourage you to share your learnings with others.

The reader is free to examine the truths, comments, or opinions being shared, to accept or reject any. Those readers who have similar experiences will readily have deeper insights into what is being stated. Those without such experiences will need time to assimilate them or may even reject them altogether as incredulous or disbelief.

Having spiritual experiences makes no one person better than another. That is just how we are created, with each person having a special mission from God on this earth. The **Freedom of our Will showered with sanctifying grace** is to choose to carry it out giving all glory to God, especially for the perfect love He shows to all of humankind.

Let us begin with John, dear reader, with an invitation to walk along the path that John traveled.

In the 1960s to the early years of the 1970s, John had reached a point in his life with a strong need to seek meanings and guidance for the experiences that he was faced with from his young years forward in the spiritual realm. Little did John know when searching for spiritual guidance that he would be walking through a spiritual and earthly upheaval of the destruction of nations, especially of his own country, the United States of America. Along the pathway, he saw many souls struggling to survive spiritually and physically throughout the world.

Disappointingly, he was faced with so much void or lack of knowledge from others, regarding dealing with spiritual experiences, especially from church leaders who one could assume would be able to help. Moreover, he was met with distain, rejection, outright ridicule, and jealousy. But he would not give up. With whatever he learnt he began to write in 1972 just to help others who were going through similar travels as he. However, it was considered too philosophical and not on the level of the regular common language for the ordinary layperson to understand. It was also presented to a bishop a decade after Vatican II when humanism, the sexual revolution, and progressivism under the disguise of relativism and collectivism took the place of spirituality, sacrifice, self-responsibility, and respect in the Church. Hence, with so much disorientation taking place in the churches and the world, John's writing was not accepted.

It was not until 2011, that J.M. Joseph wrote a book, "A Steep Climb," hoping that if John's journey was paralleled by the life of his best friend, Lou, who also was seeking his Higher Power in dealing with PTSD from serving his country as a combat soldier and medic in Korea and Viet Nam Wars, the messages of dealing with spiritual experiences could be shared with others who were walking along the same path as he and Lou were.

At the time from the 1960s to 2003, John was not able to share his experiences in-depth with Lou, the veteran, who was going through severe PTSD consisting of experiences such as: sleeping with dead bodies of the enemy in his tent because investigations were not completed and there was no- where else to put them; being exposed with his other combat army buddies in the fields of Viet Nam to agent orange by the United States, resulting in boils all over their bodies and feeling betrayed, and later in life with the seeping of blood from their body skin; the helplessness Lou felt when as a medic he kept trying to keep a Sargent alive whose back was split open and there was no chance of being saved; and atrocities including dealing with nightmares that forcefully awoke one from sleep. While going through his experiences and desperately trying to find God, Lou always stressed that War cannot be won without a plan that consisted of military and political victory. He pointed out the Wars of Viet Nam, Iraq, and if alive today, Afghanistan.

John felt it best to just be there for Lou and support him in search of his Higher Power. In the meantime, until after Lou's death, John's search in life relating to handling spiritual experiences was finally shared with Lou in memoriam, towards the end of the book in "A Steep Climb."

After the book was published in 2015-16 and re-launched in 2021, readers approached J.M. Joseph, the author of, "A Steep Climb", expressing the need to share their spiritual experiences and wanting to hear more of it.

Hence, this book will be seen through John's eyes in an altered character, and his true-life experiences from his birth in 1942 to the present and those of others who have shared their happenings. As he walks through his experiences within the surroundings that they occurred, there will be repeated elements in the surroundings that are also contained in Part I. The reader is left to see through their own eyes, the aftermaths that John and others went through and the awakenings and learnings that resulted from all the spiritual warfare and occurrences that occurred and are still taking place.

INTRODUCTION TO JOHN

I, John, being born in 1942 was brought up religiously in a church-going family. Throughout life, experiences of physical, visionary, and visitational aspects occurred. Some were extremely fearful, while others uplifted my being. I will share them and those of others as well as the learnings from many sincere persons. The important point is that when one experiences such, one walks through hell almost immediately. Questions arise. What should I do? What does it mean? What does God ask of me? How should it be handled? Obscurity sets in as one becomes forcefully exposed to two levels of existence, the natural and the spiritual or supernatural. The soul then naturally seeks out spiritual help for guidance and understanding as to how one lives on two existential levels.

It should be emphasized as J.M. Joseph just previously stated, that people who experience such will understand this in view of their own experiences. Those without experiences may doubt, some resulting in disbelief to all that is being written. And that is fine. Moreover, regardless if one has experienced or has none at all, it does not matter in God's eyes, for each individual is special and deeply loved by God.

Much of what was seen and learnt came from many diverse people, religious, other denominations, and lay people. Oral lessons shared with me by others were also later found in books. Readings verified the oral lessons and may be listed in the references. In some reference materials, I may and may not agree with all that is written.

The beginning of this Part II will review the learnings that occurred after walking along the pathway. It is no doubt that spiritual experiences push a person to seek out its meaning and the wanton of guidance to bring it to full fruition. The pull is to seek out from the highest power-God. Thus begins the walk-through hell.

WHY DOES ONE WALK THROUGH HELL WITH OR WITHOUT EXPERIENCES ON THE SPIRITUAL PLANE?

It should be noted that not only do people with spiritual experiences walk through hell, but all souls on earth do especially when reaching towards God. Those with spiritual experiences are almost immediately looking for a reason, or the meaning attached to such an experience. Thus, a strong thrust towards our God Almighty occurs. And warfare begins!

Reference to the Holy Bible, in Saint John the Apostle's Book of Revelation, Chapter 12: 7-9 will help to explain this.

"And there was war in heaven: Michael and his angels fought against the dragon, and the dragon fought and his angels,

And prevailed not; neither was their place found any more in heaven.

And the great dragon was cast out, that old serpent, called the devil, and Satan, which deceives the whole world: he was cast out into the EARTH, and his angels were cast out with him."

Common in many writings is that the fallen angels totaled to one-third.

EARTH-Guess who else is on earth? Yes, You and I, and every human being that was created with a body and soul that was born.

WHY DID SOME OF THE ANGELS CHOOSE TO FALL?

There are different versions given by many people and sources, but the two most common ones are:

1. Humans who were lower than they were going to be created by God and share in His Divine presence in Heaven. Moreover, they would have to assist humans. And it has been shared by some that those humans who are called to be saints, will judge the angels. Pride along with jealousy appeared to be the first and foremost reason.

2. Another reason shared is that God's plan was revealed that Jesus would come to earth in body and soul. And this the angels refused to worship, a God in human form, lower than they are. Again, Pride was the reason. They were not going to worship a form lower than their status.

In 1968 a Portuguese woman in her 80's, who was a healer, shared the following with me: she had a Bible when living in Portugal and she remembers reading that Jesus, while on earth, commanded Satan, who was once the highest angel in heaven, "to get off of the throne!" Being unsuccessful in finding such a writing, the following biblical passage was the closest that could be related to such:

"How art thou fallen from heaven, O Lucifer, son of the morning! How art thou cut down to the ground, which didst weakens the nations!

For thou hast said in thy heart, I will ascend into heaven, I will exalt my throne above the stars of God; I will sit also upon the mount of the congregation, in the sides of the north.

I will ascend above the heights of the clouds: I will be like the Highest.

Yet thou shalt be brought down to hell, to the sides of the pit." Isaiah 14:12-15.

WHAT IS THE AFTERMATH OF THE FALLEN THE ANGELS?

Devils, Demons

Because of the choice of their free will, the fallen angels 'main choice of purpose is to destroy and prevent as many human souls on earth from reaching out or getting close to the Blessed Trinity, to God the Father, God the Son Jesus Christ, and the Holy Spirit, from sharing in their Divine glory. They want to have the soul suffer torments, pain, and gnashing of the teeth, endlessly, eternally, and to join them because when they (fallen angels) freely chose not to accept the joyful purity of God's love and worship Him, they themselves went into eternal torment and chose to exist as such forever and be rulers of hell. So they thought.

In a sense, the war in heaven is continuing now on earth, but not against the holy angels who already won the battle in heaven with St. Michael the Archangel in the lead. Now, the warfare is against us, all humans, on earth, or whoever existed or exist with a soul. Unlike the holy angels who are pure spirits, we, humans, are of spirit and a body that is so susceptible to the vices, aroma, fragrances, and pleasures of the 7 capital sins. Therefore, with prayer, wouldn't it be also wise to call upon St. Michael the Archangel to intercede on our behalf and help us as we ward off the great temptations that aim to pull our souls into severe sinning? The fallen angels will cunningly and manipulatively go to any lengths to drag all souls downward, especially those who seek out help and guidance towards God. They want to keep as many souls as possible in endless suffering and torment in the fires of eternal hell after death. All due to their warped pride and jealously.

WHAT IS THE DIFFERENCE BETWEEN A DEMON AND A DEVIL?

There is not much of a difference. As stated previously, both are out to destroy souls that try to reach God. Some people have shared with me that demons are fallen humans and devils are fallen, angels. However, in my readings and research, some writers feel that demons are also devils and fallen angels. The only difference is that demons form closer bonds with humans in order to groom them as prey by leading them into the temptations from the world, the flesh, thereby becoming easy prey and targets for the devils.

That is why when we pray the Our Father, we end with and "lead us not into temptation (from demons), but deliver us from evil (devils)."

OUR RIGHT TO HEAVEN IS GIVEN TO EACH ONE OF US BY JESUS CHRIST

ARE THERE DIFFERENT DEGREES OF PURIFICATION OF SOULS AFTER DEATH?

JESUS CHRIST HAS COME IN THE FLESH

Apparently, there appears to be such? Common labels have been given such as Heaven, Purgatory (a level of movement for the soul as it travels to God), and Hell.

It is important to remember why Jesus Christ came to earth in the flesh. After death, there was only hell. Due to our sinfulness, Jesus Christ was conceived by the Holy Spirit, born of a virgin woman Mary, who is full of grace, and was raised to teach us as witnessed by others. He was to suffer and die for each one of us as predicted back to the first prophets, out of the Love of God the Father. In carrying out the Will of God the Father, after His death, HE DESCENDED INTO HELL to destroy the gates of hell and removed all obstacles, and released all worthy souls to move onward to heaven with His Divine Presence. HE ASCENDED INTO HEAVEN as witnessed by some followers. To this very day and in all the future of humankind, every soul who repents for their sins and follows His Divine Will has the right to enter heaven. **Jesus Christ has come in the flesh!**

What a great gift of pure love from God the Father that was and is given to each one of us through His Divine Son, Jesus Christ. Therefore, let us not lose this divine gift or fear of the Lord. No matter how many crosses we must bear or falls in life that we weaken under, let us pick up our crosses and continue on for the Lord God in forgiveness and reconciliation.

It is important to see how Jesus carried out the Will of God the Father

IS THERE A DESCRIPTION OF HELL?

Some have been given sight into it.

Our Lady of Fatima

The first part or secret revealed by Our Lady of Fatima occurred when She appeared in July, 1917 to three children. Lucia dos Santos, the oldest of the three children, and cousin to Francisco and Jacinta Marto describes it in the following manner:

When Our Lady opened her hands, "The light reflecting from them seemed to penetrate into the earth, and we saw as if into a sea of fire, and immersed in that fire were devils and souls with the human form, as if they were transparent black or bronze embers floating in the fire and swayed by the flames that issued from within themselves along with great clouds of smoke, falling upon every side just like the falling of sparks in great fires, without weight or equilibrium, amidst wailing and cries of pain and despair that horrified and shook us with terror. We could distinguish the devils by their horrible and repulsive figures of frightful and unknown animals, but transparent as the back coals in a fire.

You have seen Hell-where the souls of poor sinners go. To save them God wills to establish throughout the world the devotion to My Immaculate Heart."

In August She again mentioned that many souls are in hell because they have no one to pray for them or make sacrifices for them.

The second part called for the conversion of Russia to Her Immaculate Heart to be done on the same day by all the Catholic Bishops in the world with their congregation along with other directions that were given. Her words were: "If they heed My requests, Russian will be converted, and there will be peace. If not, she shall spread her errors throughout the world, promoting wars and persecutions of the Church; the good will be martyred, the Holy Father will have much to suffer, and various nations will be annihilated; in the end, My Immaculate Heart shall triumph. The Holy Father will consecrate Russian to Me, which will be converted, and some time of peace will be given to the world."

The third part which was to be revealed in 1960 but deliberately held back until 2000 warned about the downfall that would occur within the Church by its own church leaders. The aftermath of Vatican II proved this to be correct and up to the present time, the Catholic Church and its followers are now struggling to bring back the faith and spirituality that were removed by Masons, Marxist and Communist ideologies directed toward humanistic goals, as portrayed in Part I of this book. This part also spoke about an angel with a flaming sword, and the man dressed in white, perhaps the pope, who suffers and later is shot to death. Much of the revelation has been held back by the certain Vatican officiates. The True Story of Fatima, p.28 E-mail: info@fatima.org.com. Telephone: 1-905-871-7607

Saint Theresa of Avila

"She describes hell as a long and narrow alleyway, low dark and confined, foul stench and swarming with putrid vermin. It is the soul itself that tears itself to pieces…that interior fire and despair, in addition to extreme torments and pains…without end, never ceasing.'" A Steep Climb, J.M. Joseph, relaunch 2021, **www.writersbranding.com** p.118.

DIFFERENT DEGREES OF HELL?

It seems that there may be different degrees of hell where souls exist. Presently, we are aware that one state of being is for souls who may need to expiate for their sins on earth before entering heaven. The Catholic Church refers to one area as Purgatory. Limbo is another state of being for souls who died in the state of original sin, with nowhere to go. Then there is the state of being for souls who are satanic worshippers in the damnation of the Eternal Hell. If there are other levels or corrections needed, the Church would be able to share such with its laity.

Evidently, this is what Our Lady of Fatima requested of Christians, to pray for the souls in hell who have no one to pray to or do penance for them. Souls that may have made the wrong choice due to human frailty such as stated by Our Lady as sins of the flesh and immodest fashions, yet want to be forgiven and make some amends and don't know how to go about it yet are reaching out to find the path to God. We can all help the souls. The Mass is the strongest way to move them towards God Almighty. Prayers, such as the Rosary, are also very helpful for souls.

This is also the area that the Church finally ceased as listed in the new Compendium Catechism of the Catholic Church – www.usccbPublishing.org - to stop condemning all souls who commit suicide. Some people do so because of despair, calling for help and there is none. The problem is that after death, they are unable to help themselves as we think they could. The dilemma or dispute that they had on earth is still with them in death. It is the living that is able to help them with prayer, sacrifices, and the Holy Mass.

JUDAS ISCARIOT - Where is he?

Let us look at Judas Iscariot who was referred to, that it would be best that he was never born. One will understand this after seeing what he was faced with on this earth and after.

According to the Council of Trent, Judas is in hell. This is the apostle whom Jesus stated and referred to, that for his good, it be better that he not be born. According to the 1927 editing of Rutherford H. Platt Jr. in Lost Books of the Bible, p. 52 Bell Publishing Company, New York,

Judas was possessed as a young child and was obsessed with biting people. When playing with Jesus, he sought to bite him. But Jesus struck Judas and satan left him and entered a form of a dog that ran away. Judas, the apostle that was once possessed and released from it by Jesus, followed Jesus in later years out of love for Our Lord.

At the last supper, when all the apostles were still in wonderment and confusion as to why Jesus came and was about to do, Judas knew what he had to do. Because he loved our Lord, it was hard for him to turn Jesus over to death. But when the devil on the left shoulder enticed his free will of choice over the angel on the right shoulder, he made preparations for his betrayal of Our Lord. Evil entered him with greediness for 30 pieces of silver. Because of Judas' constant battle between good and evil, Jesus had to therefore tell him, "That thou doest, do quickly," to turn Him over to the Jews. No other apostle understood what Jesus was doing.

When Judas left to do so, Jesus Christ stated, "Now is the Son of man glorified, and God is glorified in him." John 13: 27, 31. The Divine Will of God the Father was to be carried out in its final and most crucial stages. Matthew's gospel tells us how after the betrayal, Judas realized that he had betrayed an innocent man. In turn, Judas returned the silver coins and repented. He repented. Out of despair, condemnation, and fear from others, he then hanged himself. Matthew 27:3-5. He repented.

The Apostles' Creed cites the facts of faith and states that Jesus descended into Hell. There Jesus, illuminated in His Divine light, tore open its gates and took over it entirely, releasing all the souls that died in grace and repentance and doing expiation for their sins. Could Judas be one to have gone up to Jesus, an apostle that fell into deep deadly sin, realized that he did wrong and repented and then committed suicide? He probably did expiate for his sins asking for forgiveness? If so, what would Jesus have done? You, dear reader, draw your own conclusion. Moreover, Our Lady of Fatima keeps asking for prayers and penance for souls in hell that want to be saved but need help.

It seems that Judas was in warfare from the time he was born. He was possessed as a youngster, freed of it by Jesus, followed Jesus later in life, and then again fell into evil along with the betrayal of Christ. He then realized he did wrong, repented, and out of despair committed suicide. Till today, he has been despised, hated, and condemned to Hell by generations after generations, up into the 21^s Century. That probably was meant as to why it would have been better if he was not born. People have condemned him to the eternal fires of Hell for endless years. However, he may be the greatest saint in heaven today without any of us knowing; that is if he asked for forgiveness and was released from Hell when Jesus descended there and ruled over it.

WHO OR WHAT GETS INTERTWINED IN ALL OF THE WARFARE?

Let us look at the hierarchy of existence, whether spiritual, intellectual, or material:

GOD	Infinite Spirit	JESUS
ANGELS	Angelic Spirit	
HUMANS	Human Spirit with a Body	JESUS
ANIMALS	Animal Consciousness and Body	
PLANTS	Plant Consciousness and Body	
NON-LIVING	Consciousness and matter	

Notice that HUMANS down to NON-LIVING occupy EARTH along WITH the fallen angels. But in the spiritual realm, God is the highest, then the angels and the humans are the lowest. The importance of JESUS is seen in His Godly Divinity as the second person of the Blessed Trinity. Then He is depicted by His Cross as a human on earth, and as the connector between Heaven, Earth, and Hell with His Resurrection when He has set us FREE for all eternity.

As St. John, the young apostle stated, "Jesus Christ has come in the flesh." I. John 4:2

WHY ARE ANIMALS, PLANTS, AND NONLIVING SEEN WITH CONSCIOUSNESS IN THE HIERARCHY OF EXISTENCE?

Different degrees of reactions are observed in these levels.

Animals

Humankind has advanced with more insights into many things with the latest scientific research and studies. Many pet owners will share how their animals (dogs, cats, birds, fish, etc.) do understand and learn some human functions such as, when to press certain buttons to relay their thoughts to their owners, being cognizant of when their owner is ill or in danger, and yes, showing anger or jealousy when needed. Even fish know when to behave and when to attack other fish to get their way. Behavior modification works with humans and animals.

Plants

Science projects by students and adults have proven to show how plants react to music, growing healthier with soothing music as compared to loud rock sounds.

Non-Living Matter

Someone shared with me about a professor in Japan who did excellent studies on nonliving matter-water. Water crystals were deformed when the water was exposed to pollutants, dirt, and even loud rock music. The water crystals were beautiful with 6-sided flakes when it was clean water or exposed to soothing music. Non-living can react to the environment.

HOW THEN DOES A PERSON WALK THROUGH THE HELL OF WARFARE?

It is stated by many that humans must be aware of **the temptations of the world, the flesh, and the devil** who can also appear as an angel of light. And while we deal with some from the natural level, we need to remember that our **battle is really with the principalities and powers of evil,** as we all share the same EARTH.

"For we wrestle not against (only) flesh and blood, but against principalities, against powers, against the rulers of the darkness of this world, against spiritual wickedness in high places," (air-spirits). Ephesians 6:12.

IS THIS THE RESULT ONLY OF THE FALLEN ANGELS OR OF ORIGINAL SIN OR PERHAPS BOTH?

The free choice made by Adam and Eve in the Book of Genesis seemed to satisfy the evil force in the Garden of Eden. Their choice matched the free choice made by the fallen angels. One must remember as stated in Part I of this book, that when Adam was commanded directly by God to not eat the forbidden fruit, Eve was not yet created. When the devil aimed at and tempted Eve, although being somewhat aware that a command was given to Adam, she was deceived and sinned. Adam, who was standing by her, said nothing to stop her and was not deceived when he sinned. Yet he places the blame on Eve. Eve, in turn, blames the serpent, and later, because of her love for Adam, took all the blame entirely. Thus, with the lack of accountability and responsibility on the part of both of them, came the downfall of possibly, the 7 capital sins that intertwine on the levels of existence that promote this battle on earth.

So, looking back at the levels in the hierarchy of existence from the angels down to the non-living, one can see how they can cause injury to souls when infested with the 7 capital sins from which other sins flow. Each individual has a cross to bear for God, some more than one cross.

Here is a list of the 7 capital sins:

Pride - excessive ambition, vanity, use of lies or demeaning others to serve oneself as opposed to humility

Covetousness - to take what is rightfully not yours

Lust - desires that result in the love of self at other's expense, excessive desires

Anger - emotions beyond control that result in murders, quarrels, hurting others

Gluttony - excessiveness in all areas, speaking, eating, drinking, power, greed, and other appetites

Envy - taking joy in destroying other's fortunes in various ways

Sloth - neglect of what should be done, omitting what ought to be maybe due to fear, etc.

Results: drug and alcohol abuse, murders, lies resulting in insurrections and killings of innocent people, stealing, divorces, pornography, sex trafficking, abuses and harassment on the jobs, in the families, gangs, with animals, and the plant environment, curses, relations with evil, satanic cults that drains the mind, body, and souls of their energy and connection to God, seen even in satanic psychic cults, etc. and the list goes on. Don't these all read the same as in Part I, in ways to destroy or annihilate a nation that knows peace and keep it in the chains of hell?

Great atrocities, violence, and ravaging in historic episodes have resulted when human behaviors are worse than that of animals. Again, one only needs to research on Wars, the Crusades-Crusaders, Arabs, Muslims, Papacy, Slavery, Germany's Hitler and the extermination of the Jews, ethnic cleansing, Slavery, a documentary on The Rape of Nanking by Iris Chang, and other damnable happenings in the history of humans.

Abusive and un-natural human actions such as: the rape of men, women, and children of all ages, disempowerment, the mutilations of the bodies of the living and dead, boiling of live humans and eating of them (cannibalism), setting them on fire while alive after lusting after their bodies and other actions will reveal the inhumane and diabolical side of humans that goes way beyond that of the animal kingdom, being in mutual agreement with the fallen angels and the flip of the hierarchy of existence takes place. It then becomes:

GOD   JESUS
ANGELS
HUMANS   JESUS
ANIMALS
PLANTS
NON-LIVING
HUMANS & FALLEN ANGELS - a living hell on earth

But those *HUMANS* who hold on to their faith of love of God, respect for human dignity, and love of neighbor and God's creations, remain between the angels and animals in the hierarchy.

Yes, there is Jesus, for the freedom of the human will to reach out to.

All of these hellish aspects previously mentioned need not be so profound and destructive. With the graces from God, we need to choose to fight the best we can, in carrying our cross or crosses in our warfare battles to move towards our Almighty Creator by living in the state of divine graces, with the help of all of the sacraments, sacramentals, doctrines, the Ten Commandments, Acts of Mercy, the Beatitudes, increasing the degree of the Gifts of the Holy Spirit, prayer especially the Rosary, etc. at our disposal. Thus, the importance of the responsibility of all churches on earth to minister to their flocks in what was taught and revealed by Jesus Christ who has come in the flesh.

Ultimately, it is the **love of God in one's heart and soul and love of neighbor** that bring the human soul to its rightful heights, on earth, and to heaven. No one is perfect and as such one must not be blasphemous against the Holy Spirit and judge the soul of his neighbor. But do judge the human action or choice of behavior. Someone could have committed theft due to being so desperate and unable to find a job despite all sincere efforts made, in order to feed his family. That is why it is truly a warfare.

CAUTION: EVIL APPEARING AS AN ANGEL OF LIGHT

We, humans, are easily tricked in this area. God and the church are used by many to accomplish their self-serving goals. This is what is meant when the following is referred to: appearing as an angel of light, or the wolf appeared in sheep clothing. There are many examples but if you recall in Part I:

A politician brain-washes his followers with lies that at a point in time resulted in an insurrection where innocent lives were threatened and lost; in the meantime, the person is abusive and demeans those who do not agree with him and treats the opposite gender in the same manner. The clincher here is when this politician declared a platform that is pro-life, so many churches and ministers, and Christians fell quickly in line to back the candidate up, forgetting that the father of lies is the devil.

Another politician treats others with human dignity, looking out for the good of all, and is pro-choice. The churches and ministers and some Christians immediately condemn this candidate because of being pro-choice, whereby allowing a person to freely choose, either way, to do or not to do the killing of an unborn.

This is where the purpose of the church on earth comes in, **to teach, preach, and live the way of Jesus Christ for Christians and others to follow in the Reality of Life,** in order that people will make the right choice. It is important to remember that God **the Father** gave humans the **gift of the freedom of the will to choose, as well as the separation of the church and state which was made clear by JESUS.**

Whatever factor lies in one's way of life, the individual is free to choose good.

When this candidate won the election, one ministry stated that the other candidate was being shown humility by God. Moreover, some bishops of the catholic church wanted to deny the winning candidate the reception of the Holy Eucharist. **Not one admitted being deceived by the devil who appeared as an angel of light.**

Were these two candidates used to bring the churches, ministers, clergy, Christians, and others back to their senses? Great possibility!

Regarding EARTH, **Pastor Riley stated it so succinctly," We humans are just passing through EARTH! We are not meant to be here forever. We don't belong here." Therefore, let us make the most of it and bring many souls to God Almighty while on EARTH.**

LET THE SHARING OF EXPERIENCES BEGIN

The Power of Prayer

A. As a young child, I was very sickly. Back in those days, there was no effective treatment for severe asthma attacks, no vaccines, no inhalers, no ventilators or vaccinations, nothing except a little black pill that tasted so sour upon one's tongue. For over a year, whenever an attack came, and quite frequently, the doctor would arrive at the house in the middle of the night, sometimes at 10 p.m., at midnight, at 1:00 or 2:00 am, and all that was done was to lift me up high with his arms and call out, "Breathe, Breathe, Breathe!" After continuously gasping, and struggling to push air into my lungs I would succumb to unconsciousness, giving up due to sheer, total emotional and physical exhaustion. This occurred time and time again.

Besides the doctor, others thought many times that survival was difficult and that death would be imminent. But having loving and prayerful parents who reached out to Our Heavenly Father, the Lord saw otherwise and kept me on this earth. As time went by and in my late teen years, antibiotics and inhalers and good old Vicks Vapor Rub came to the rescue. But it really was **the power of prayer** that kept me alive till then and even till today. Little did I know, that this was the beginning of my warfare on earth. From then on, I was always sickly throughout my life. But God is always so loving and kind.

B. In another case, a young girl had a bad rash on the abdominal area of her body. Many doctors were sought for treatment and nothing seemed to work. It appeared that there was no medicine to help with its removal. Her parents then turned to our Almighty God with prayer, and finally, through His Divine Grace, complete healing took place. **The power of prayer.** Today, there would be more choices at hand for treatments due to the advancement in scientific research in the fields of medicine, such as Biochemistry and other areas. At that time, not much was known, and faith in God overturned culture and pulled many people through tough times in health.

Importance of Christianity VS. Demonic cultural practices

Having had an interest in a medical career in order to save the lives of others from suffering, at age 13, advice was sought from my medical doctor. He came to our area after completing his medical training and some years of practice. Having acclimated to the culture and climate he medically served our people for many years. There was no doubt that he was elated to find that he had such an influence on my future career.

He shared various treatments that he used to cure people. However, he stated with much sadness that there were certain but few cases that could not be cured. These cases were due to evil cultural practices. It was unfortunate that Christianity was not deeply practiced or known in the early days of such a culture.

As within all cultures, there are demonic practices that are seen as acceptable because of being desensitized as a normal cultural practice. Many different practices in various cultures were then made known to me such as people calling upon spirits from the dead to carry out evil intentions, people adoring evil spirits in sticks, rocks, and other items, and feeding them in order to carry out their personal demonic intentions and others. If it is not taken care of, it turns its evil upon its owner.

It was clear that there was a lack of knowing God Almighty, knowing and feeling His Divine Love in our hearts and souls as to why His Son,

Jesus Christ has come in the flesh. Again, the free will of an individual comes into play. A deeper awakening of the importance of having the Lord God in one's life began. Devoted and sincere Missionaries who put God first and not sought to steal from the infancy of their believers, are to be thanked for spreading God's Word.

Vision in a dream

It was also at this time that a spiritual vision was granted in a dream. The good Lord, Jesus Christ, was enraptured in all the beauty of white-yellowish heavenly glow that illuminated brightly as He came downward towards me upon a cloud. He was sitting upon a golden throne, draped in his white garment with a red overthrow over His shoulder and a golden crown upon His head.

It remained above the ground, higher than where I was standing. The brilliant glow of His face was such that I could not see His features clearly except for a little of His brownish head hair faded by the light's illumination. Being enraptured by its spiritedness, somehow, I strongly knew that He smiled as He blessed me with His Hand. After a while, He ascended gently upward towards heaven until it all disappeared. It was so very beautiful. A feeling of being uplifted resulted from this soul-rapturing experience. And I thought many people must have similar dreams and that it was a common thing. Later, there was wonderment as to what does it all mean?

Then a walk-through hell followed.

Negative presence of a being in a semi-conscious state of sleep: the HOLY NAME OF JESUS

After having such a beautiful vision, as time went by, experiences of the opposite nature occurred. Upon the threshold of awakenings, there would be a clear sense of a being close by that would overcome me with fear. It could be felt spiritually and very few times somewhat physically, and a strong sense that it was of an evil nature penetrated the surroundings. It would leave me paralyzed and helpless and so very fearful, that I would dare not want to try to open my eyes. And I knew and felt that it couldn't open even if tried. From the depth of my soul, I would call out to Jesus, His Holy Name, JESUS! JESUS! And then a deep sleep of slumber would overcome me. A normal awakening would follow later on. This happened many, many times over quite a number of years, even through the adult years. Being ignorant of such and not liking it, I just simply thought that it was something that had to be dealt with. There may be others who also have to deal with such.

VATICAN II

Vatican II took place in 1962, a grandiose event that would affect every nation and every corner of the earth including heaven and hell. Instead of revealing the 3rd Secret of Our Lady of Fatima as asked by Her, changes in the name of progressivism in order to modernize Christianity began to eat away at the spiritual hierarchy level of Christianity. Contrary to immediately correcting falsehoods within the church, such as condemning all souls who committed suicide to hell, most initial efforts brought the church down in appeasing humanity.

After relinquishing a medical path to being a teacher in a religious school, one could see the humanistic and technological approach that the wave of progressivism was heading, moving away from spiritualism, suffering, and sacrifice for God to the pleasing of oneself.

Vision while fully awake

Once again God Almighty granted another vision in 1968, but this time I was fully awake. I was riding in the car with someone and happened to look out the window at the sky. Lo and behold there was my image in the sky, exactly as I was sitting there in the car looking up. Many tortured souls were behind of my image, with their faces and heads twisted and pulled in all directions, expressing much pain and internal suffering. So much torment was seen in their faces. On the left stood our Blessed Mother, Mary Immaculate, Our Lady of Grace, looking at my normal image with the suffering faces of souls behind me. Rays of lights and graces streaming from Her hands were seen. Her face glowed with the white light clouds of heaven and it was thought that it may be just an image. I kept looking away and checking to see if it was still there and not due to my imagination. Back and forth, repeatedly, I kept looking away, even rubbing my eyes, and still, the vision was there. And then it began to change. In its final stage, a monk in his long habit with the hood covering his head, appeared, holding an open book in his hands. This portion then ended after a while. With all the checking and re-checking, I knew it was real without any doubt.

Not a word was spoken, just the images in the white clouds clear as daylight, every image articulately and accurately formed. No clear faces were seen, as the whiteness of the heavenly light faded features with its glow. Only my facial image was seen in its normal, clear form, along with the tortured Souls in the background, Our Holy Mother, and then the Monk. And there was not one sound from the driver who did not notice a single thing. And again, it was thought that many people or everybody experiences visions on a spiritual plane.

A realization existed that a vision can be seen by one person even if more people are present. Even though there was no understanding of this vision at that time, there was a strong yearning to know and search out its meaning. Somehow there was a deep feeling and wonderment that something was being asked of me. I did not know what to do but could only pray upon it. But that deep pull within to start searching lingered onward.

The writings of St. Thomas Aquinas verified that visions can be seen by individuals.

Many years later, as I conversed with a person of faith, it was thought that perhaps the monk was St. Jerome or another monk. To this day I do not know. But the vision drew me to read the Bible whenever and where ever; at home, on a trip, in a doctor's office, etc. And like many of you know, the same passage could be read time and time again, and the meanings attained can be different from the previous ones. The history and cultures were referred to for deeper meanings. And these were areas that were referred to as the Bible was taught in high school. It was after many years, after pushing aside the cultural and historical facts to their proper place, did the love of God and why Jesus Christ came in the flesh was made clearer.

The images of tortured souls whose heads and facial features were twisted in agonizing pain moved me to the message of Our Lady of Fatima. Pray for the souls in hell that have no one to pray for them. Souls that made a wrong choice, but do love God.

Another walk-through hell occurred.

Negative presence of a being while fully awake-The Power of the HOLY NAME OF JESUS CHRIST in the battle of spirits

One evening at twilight time, another negative event was experienced. Unlike before, this time I was fully awake. Sitting on a comfortable chair while reading a book of interest provided so much relaxation. It was not to last. Suddenly, deep harsh breathing sounds were heard. It came closer and closer in my direction as I continued to quietly read my book. It got louder and louder as it reached almost by the side of the chair. Paralyzed with a deep fear that overtook me, I could not even call out to the other person in the room. A frozen state entirely overtook me. Again, feeling a loss as to how to handle such, my spirit alone was all that I had to fight off that evil spirit. From the depth of my soul, with all the strength of my spirit, I called out in my true spirit form, the Holy Name of JESUS! JESUS!…. And it stopped…. and left. It was my spirit against another spirit.

Later on in life, after reading the works of St. John of the Cross, I understood with fullness what he meant when he stated how dealing with evil can include spirit against the spirit. The fear produced rises above all sensory pain. This memory remains with you throughout life.

Prayer and receiving the Holy Eucharist were all that I had to assist me at that time.

WAS SPIRITUAL HELP SOUGHT? SHARING OF EXPERIENCES CONTINUE

It was by this time that I knew I needed spiritual help, someone to guide me in understanding what these experiences mean and what I should do, especially if God is asking me to do something. A new journey in life began.

Priest, ministers, religions, and those who dedicated their lives to the service of God were the first that were sought out. In the 1960s these servants of God were held with the utmost reverence by Christians and others as they were supposing to be examples of spiritual holiness. Whatever they said to do, we Christians throughout the world would do without question. And as a teacher in a religious school that is the path that was taken.

A very dedicated priest whom I knew welcomed my visit with him in the latter 60s. As I started to explain the reason for my visit to discuss visions, trying to find meaning in them, and without a chance to share also the negative side of fear and how to handle such, he quickly grabbed my shoulders and quietly ushered me out of his office, whispering to me, "Don't talk about it to anyone, don't mention it, keep quiet about it, just trust in God." After the door closed, I just stood there outside of his office feeling so lost and empty. Today, the realization is that many were perhaps treated in the same manner. Others who also sought spiritual help during these years also shared the same treatment given them and may have felt lost or rejected.

Other efforts that were made to seek a spiritual guide were met with laughter, slide remarks as being mentally unstable, emotionally disturbed, and imaginative, and also resulted in the avoidance and sometimes the loss of so-called friends. I was even called an atheist. That is being stated with much humor! It was then made clear to me as why the priest gave me the warning about keeping quiet and not telling anyone. He must have gone through this dark path also. It also revealed clearly how instead of addressing the needed advice or spiritual guidance for souls, there was a tendency of some priests, ministers, and others to look for or point out the faults of a soul.

I did wonder why was there no priest that would understand and sit with me to direct me as to what was needed. At that time, I lacked the understanding and knowledge of what priests themselves lacked as well as what was happening with so many changes occurring within the church and world. Many Christians were going through many changes. We just followed through as lambs being led to the slaughter.

Another holy priest stated that there is no such thing as spiritual experiences. It can all be proven through science. And I pondered, but God is Science. This made me all the more assertive to test anything that may occur. I had to keep seeking.

It was also shown at this time that warfare can be strong, accompanied by temptations, confusion, and anything to offset a soul from seeking God. Indeed, it is a time for prayer, receiving the sacraments, using sacramentals such as medals, and asking God for His Divine Protection for yourself and especially those dear to you. These are important steps to take. **Warfare has moments of intensity at times.**

Pity the woman who goes through such at this time. She would be smothered to the ground, as gender equality was not seen or practiced as it should have been in every aspect of life, businesses, politics, medical, educational, labor, military, and other fields, even within the circles of churches. The Bible, which presents just a few women in content, and at least the most important one, the Mother of Jesus, plays a part in how a woman was and is looked upon.

Part of the old Jewish culture, that is seen in the Bible does not help also. Unless one sees and interprets the respect and love of Jesus and God for womanhood, just reading the words of the Bible can lead to misinterpretation and ideas of misogamy due to many cultural biases.

WHEN DID BIASES AGAINST WOMEN BEGIN? A repeat of part I

Most people for generations would trace such biases as stemming from and depicted in the story of creation in the Book of Genesis, written in an etymological style of writing while lacking science. It begins with Adam being created first, and then Eve

Let us examine this etymology version as depicted in Genesis closer:

Adam was given directly by God the command to not eat the fruit before Eve was created.

Eve was deceived by the devil knowing somehow yet not clearly of the command and ate the fruit while Adam was present.

Adam was not deceived and did not stop Eve in her transgression as he stood by her side.

His action is therefore equal to her transgression. Both share in equal transgressions simply by the freedom of their own individual will. They failed to stop each other.

As a result, they fell from a preternatural of great aura existence to the natural more sensual plane. However, they still retained their spiritual souls along with their bodies.

Looking at what happened with clear lenses:

Adam, who was not deceived, hides behind Eve and blames her. Eve, still deceived and blinded by irresponsible love, blames the devil. A book titled THE FORGOTTEN BOOKS OF EDEN, edited by Rutherford H. Platt, Jr. in 1927, Bell Publishing Company, New York contains writings from before and after the death of Jesus Christ. In ADAM AND EVE V: 4-5, p. 7, Eve takes full blame to cover up for Adam after feeling extremely downhearted because of the great blame that Adam manipulatively placed upon her. This bias of irresponsible behaviors of unequal transgressions on the part of both Adam and Eve has been indoctrinated for centuries within the churches that flowed outward in all aspects of life.

Most importantly, it is here that God foretold to the serpent devil, the coming of our Holy Mother, Mary Immaculate, and His Divine Son, Jesus: "And I will put enmity between thee and the woman, and between they seed and her seed; it shall bruise thy head, and thou shall bruise his heel."

GENESIS 2:16-25, 3:1-20

Other biblical passages that have been preached in biased states for centuries by many preachers who were primary males, who also started up churches (as stated in a newspaper article) are quoted here:

"Let a woman learn in silence with full submissiveness. I do not permit a woman to teach or to exercise authority over a man, but to be in silence. For Adam was formed first, then Eve. Also, Adam was not deceived, but the woman was thoroughly deceived and came to be in transgression. However, she will be kept safe through childbearing, provided they continue in faith and love and sanctification along with soundness of mind."

1 TIMOTHY 2:11-15

In another passage from St. Paul, who even with his Jewish cultural background, tries to combine it with the teaching of Christ.

"Submitting yourselves one to another in the fear(love) of God. Wives, submit yourselves unto your own husbands, as unto the Lord.

For the husband is the head of the wife, even as Christ is the head of the church: and he is the savior of the body.

Therefore, as the church is subject unto Christ, so let the wives be unto their own husbands in everything.

Husbands, love our wives, even as Christ also loved the church and gave himself for it.

That he might sanctify and cleanse it with the washing of water by the word.

That he might present it to himself a glorious church, not having spot, or wrinkle, or any such thing but that it should be holy and without blemish.

So, ought men to love their wives as their own bodies. He that loveth his wife loveth himself.

For no man ever yet hated his own flesh; but nourisheth and cherisheth it, even as the Lord the church: For we are members of his body, of his flesh, and of his bones.

For this, the cause shall a man leave his father and mother and shall be joined unto his wife, and they two shall be one flesh.

This is a great mystery: but I speak concerning Christ and the church.

Nevertheless, let every one of you in particular so love his wife even as himself; and the wife see that she reverence her husband."

EPHESIANS 5:21-33

One would have hoped that Vatican II would have concentrated on correcting the biased teachings of the church in order to bring all souls (male and female) closer to God and not bending to please the pleasures of humankind that can easily lead to abuse between the genders. A wonderful and dedicated priest, Father Christopher K. 2022, put it succinctly: "God created Eve from the side of Adam." Therefore, both were created by God. For this reason, both are to live and work together side by side, helping and supporting one another. There is no excuse for abuse! And in the vows of Holy Matrimony, remember the commitment, in sickness (mental, physical, etc.) and in health, (you must help one another with love) until death do us part." This priest defended all sacraments as they were meant to be, executing the vows he took in Holy Orders in all holiness in glorifying God.

One woman seeking spiritual help at this time shared how a Brother in a Religious Congregation stated to her about the importance of Adam being the first human created and that the holy spirit operates through the penis of a male. He was ranting that since Eve was taken from his rib, it referred to the bone from the penis. He later asked the woman if he could see her genitals.

Approximately, forty years later, this thinking was released in a Netflix movie, THE KEEPERS, whereby a nun who was trying to protect sexually abused female students from priests, particularly one priest, brothers, and others who were associated with the clergy, was killed. One of the students who attended the all-girls school in Baltimore, Maryland, stated how she was told by this sexual priest predator the same obnoxious statement about receiving the holy spirit through his genitals. Sister Cathy was killed in 1969. How in the world did this concept travel all across the continent, over the ocean to where this woman lived? Evidently, at that time, there existed a pipeline within the church spreading this concept.

Another dedicated priest at the beginning of the 70s did try to help me by reading from a book about visions written by a Frenchman. The author wrote about the different types of visions. In any event, it was apparent that this priest had no deep understanding of what he was reading, but his intention and efforts were sincere and I took it to heart and was thankful for his effort and help. There may have been laughter in the monastery that evening.

With continual prayer, an outreach to others besides religious who would understand about spiritual experiences was made. It was within the realm of the lay people that relief was given outwardly with deep faith in God.

THE SPREAD OF COMMUNISM-DEALING WITH FREEDOM FOR A STUDENT

In the very early years of 1970, as the start of a new school day began with the opening of the classroom windows in preparation for welcoming the students, the principal appeared at the fifth-grade classroom doorway with a student of Asian ethnicity.

"This is your new student from China, who just arrived, John." Taking me aside, in a low tone of voice he uttered that this student was taken in the middle of the night from his home by his uncle at the request of his parents who were going to be arrested and tortured by the communistic Red Guards for their belief in democracy. The boy appeared shaken, with tears in his eyes, missing his parents. Not a word of English did he speak. However, with the support from his fellow students and school staff, he began to speak quite well in no time at all and did very well in his studies.

No one knew that in the year 2022, democracy in America would be at stake, due to a political party and its followers that were heading towards an authoritarian government, knowingly or unknowingly.

WHEN IS A VISION OR VISITATION GIVEN BY GOD?

A Christian couple, so close to the Lord God, who also exorcised, (I thought only priests could exorcise, but when there is none, the laity needs to come forth and battle upfront) shared how to detect whether a vision is God-sent or not.

Vision: The key is when a vision draws a person closer to God or even helps other souls to move closer to God, it is of a holy nature.

Visitations: Like cases similar to Aunty Tina and Sam in the latter part of this section, and others, in dealing with visitations, let us refer to the first book by J.M. Joseph, A Steep Climb:

St. John's Gospel tells us to test all spirits, living and dead with the question, "Has Jesus Christ come in the Flesh?" The spirit who responds with positive energy or acknowledges such knows that by His Cross and Resurrection, Jesus Christ came to earth, was crucified, and died to open the gates of hell for souls to go to heaven. Jesus now holds the power over all of hell even where all that is evil is damned to the eternal portion because of their own free choice to be damned there for all eternity.

If the visitation is not from God or NOT granted with permission from Our Heavenly Father, it will be a fearful and unpleasant visitation, with anger, aggressiveness, depression, threatening atmosphere, and may include other negative aspects. One must then rebuke such a vision or visitation in the Holy Name of Jesus Christ!

As in the first book of A Steep Climb, St. Theresa of Avila exemplified the use of Holy Water to dispel evil. Fatima Center sends out leaflets that state one can also use a blessed ST. Benedict Medal, Holy Water, Blessed Salt, or Blessed Candles.

An important reminder: we need to watch what we ask for. It is said that we should not ask for visions or visitations, etc. If it is meant to be, let God give it in God's time and according to His Holy Will. Remember Newton's law that we learnt in elementary grades, for every action there is an opposite and equal reaction. This holds true with visions and visitations. It is seen in the life of saints as well. One walks through hell before or after a holy vision or visitation. But it is a holy walk-through hell, regardless of all the bashing you take, for the love of God is in leading others to God through Jesus Christ. Jesus walks along or carries you through it all.

The Christian couple and many ministers from other denominations shared their learnings orally and through writings as well. By 1972, it became necessary to write what I learnt from others through God's guidance in order to help other souls who needed guidance until they could find their own spiritual director. After sharing the writing with a few people, it was thought that it was written more in a philosophical style. A few suggested that it be written using more common language terminology. It was resumed in later years.

Ending the Semi Conscious States of fear due to the Presence of Negativity: My Holy Anger and Rebuke in Jesus' Name

The search continued for spiritual guidance. Having to deal with the semi-sleep stage of paralysis with fear continued until one day when the wife of the spiritual couple sat in conversation with me. The years of experiencing fear were shared. With no hesitation, she succinctly stated in a commanding voice, "Have no fear. Open your eyes, force them to open, and confront it, rebuke it in Jesus' name."

When it happened again, with much **holy anger** that gave me the courage **to push fear aside**, I forced my eyes to open and confront it and called out the holy name of "JESUS", rebuked it, and immediately it faded and stopped. It **finally ended after all those years** of fear, a weapon of anything demonic.

That is why the Holy Name of JESUS CHRIST should always be used with great reverence, belief, and love, never in swearing, or any negative usage.

LEARNING TO DEAL WITH SPIRITUAL EXPERIENCES THROUGH THE SAINTS

There is much deep gratitude to be given to the nuns, the sisters of the Sacred Hearts of Jesus and Mary, and the Dominican nuns. They shared so much about dealing with temptations, and the importance of prayers, and moved me to read books on spiritual growth like The Soul of the Apostolate by Dom Jean-Baptiste Chautard, O.C.S.O, and on the Saints, especially books containing the writings of St. Teresa of Avila, Dark Night of the Soul by St. John of the Cross, Padre Pio, and others. These saints dealt with many spiritual experiences and shared how to handle the evilness and how to live daily by helping others to God. These writings of the saints would help anyone seeking God or walking through warfare towards the holiness of God.

In addition, just being in the presence of these nuns, one is immediately feeling and seeing the dedication and commitment of their vows in action, in being examples of what it means to serve God, through obedience, poverty, and chastity, their lives in celibacy as the priests, giving all of their being to the glory of God. Of course, they too, as with priests, are human and subject to falls. But without hesitation, and clinging to the grace of God, they immediately pick up their cross or crosses and move on, always walking to the Divine.

Once again, within the readings of St. John of the Cross, I understood exactly what he meant when he stated about the battle between spirit and spirit. It is a frightening experience for a newcomer, an event that remains throughout one's life on earth.

As previously stated, it was later on in life that an affirmation came from the writings of St. Thomas Aquinas, book titled Basic Writings of St. Thomas Aquinas by Anton C. Pegis, Random House, New York 1945. P. 107-108, that an individual can have a vision without others seeing it also, contrary to what other writers have stated.

GROWTH OF TECHNOLOGY

It was during the years of the 1950- 60s that technology was on the rise. Early one morning in a science class lecture in the latter part of the 1960s, I stated to my students that we should be ethical in how technology is developed and used. It is important to know what we ought or ought not to do, not to destroy but to assist human life, for according to Newton's laws, for every action there is an opposite and equal reaction. It came back to me that a berating to my students was made by a priest as to what I said to them. It was as if technology could do no wrong. No-fault to this priest as he was very devoted to God. He may have been captivated by the newness of the technology and the wonders that it could do, a reaction that many of us also shared. However, perhaps he did not see other levels of consequences that could result from it at that time but did so later on.

About seven years later, this devoted priest, Fr. Thomas C. saw the supreme and sublime importance of God in our lives and worked to promote the sanctity and blessedness of the Holy Eucharist and the Adoration of the Blessed Sacrament. Because of his holy priestly efforts, many souls are being nourished and saved with the Adoration of the Blessed Sacrament, a peaceful time with the Lord.

Regarding Newton's law: for every action, there is an opposite and equal reaction. We see this in how we use technology. With all of the solar panels used as an alternative source of energy, especially in a crowded acreage, we have birds falling from the sky partly roasted or more. Wind turbines have similar results, with birds being caught in their blades. This awakens us to be prepared to lessen the opposite reactions that can occur as we advance in science, technology, and other areas that affect our lives.

The Love and Power of Jesus Christ

Wanting to learn more about the Jewish Seder Meal as a teacher, I looked forward to attending one in the early 1980s. It was held by a group of Jewish believers that now included Jesus Christ in their religion, a new movement that was taking place on a small scale. James, a young adult sat next to me. As we were partaking of the bitter herbs consisting of parsley and other greens, we started up a conversation as to where we worked and the reason why we were attending this event. After sharing with James that my intent was to learn and appreciate his religion, he then shared his reason as to why he was there.

With a little hesitation, and wondering if he could trust me, James then began to share that as a teen he was deeply involved with the abuse of drugs. Crystal meth, marijuana, cocaine, LSD, and date drugs, were some of the drugs so easily available at that time as long as you had the money for them. James then blurted out about the fear that he was faced with when he was confronted by demons and devils. Deep within himself, he heard about Jesus Christ. He called upon Jesus Christ when he was faced with so much diabolical fear and the presence of its source. **And Jesus heard his desperate cry for help.** His life was changed around and he now confesses his belief in Jesus Christ in his Jewish faith.

A sudden un-natural force-the Power of Faith and Prayer

One evening as the sun finally set and darkness covered the earth, a spiritual friend and I sat at the white kitchen table in a house that was rented, talking about faith and the churches. It was a quiet evening, no wind, no sounds around us, very serene and peaceful. Suddenly, in a split second, and without any warning, the kitchen door swiftly and with full force swung open and slammed against the wall with tremendous sound! No one was there! All surroundings continued to stand still and the sound of the door ceased. It felt a little uncomfortable and just a little shaken as we sat there trying to make sense of what just happened. The spiritual friend sat calmly and prayed in a peaceful manner to which I joined in. "People who lived here before did something not good," she muttered and prayed over a certain part of the rented house. All was then calmed again.

Oh, the power of faith and prayer!

DID THIS DEPICT THE NEED FOR GOD'S MINISTERS, HIS HEAVENLY AND EARTHLY WARRIORS TO BE ARMED FOR BATTLE? Brief review from Part I

St. Michael, Where are You?

The changes of progressivism from Vatican II affected many throughout our global world. The prayer asking God for St. Michael to protect us from all evil was removed at the end of Mass. We were left on our own to seek his help. Other changes resulting from Vatican II were challenging that also intertwined with the changes in the church, education, society, and family life. Some were fine but most strongly moved toward the pleasure of humans and pushed spiritually into the background. The need for St. Michael the Archangel came into strong focus following post-Vatican II.

Sensitivity Training

In the post-Vatican II latter 1960s years, we were mandated as employees in Catholic Schools to attend professional training. Part of our training as teachers in a religious school was to attend conferences that would make us effective and better teachers for the sake of our students, in curriculum or instruction. So, we thought. This was our first exposure to Sensitivity Training. We were deliberately divided into encounter groups to release our inhibitions. If we felt like swearing with vulgarity to anyone in the group that was fine and were asked to go ahead and do so. If we wanted to touch someone in any way, place, or fashion, that was fine. If we just wanted to say anything to a person, out of love, out of anger, with vulgarity, regardless of their feelings, that was fine. Let it all hang out was somewhat of a slogan. Moving forward without any inhibitions was its underlying theme. Many attendees cringed at this sudden attempt to remove our behavioral values and moral values that we were taught from our young years and up in the spiritual as well as the physical areas.

Needless to say, we were stunned, shocked, and wondered how could we be exposed to such training from leaders of the church that was in complete opposite to our beliefs in loving God and our neighbors with respect, decency, and integrity, besides our professional training as educators. We were immediately aware that in releasing inhibitions, the decreasing and destruction of normal human and spiritual values would take place.

As this type of training spread especially among the clergy and religious, swear words and their vulgarity were being accepted into normal daily communications. The shadowing and gradual disappearance of values in all aspects of life began to occur. Spiritual guidance on spiritual experiences was difficult to find. I had to keep searching.

When visited by a priest from another congregation, we teachers were told proudly that he swore, smoked, and partied with the people he ministered to in order to make them feel that he was one of them. And we thought to ourselves, then who will be a role model for them to follow in the footsteps of Christ; who would show them respect, humility, and values in life? However, this enlightened me as to what type of God's minister, especially a priest, to look out for and select as a spiritual guide.

Unfortunately, it was not only among the staff members in religious schools that encountered groups with sensitivity training took place. It was practiced heavily in catholic seminaries throughout the world and introduced into universities, the business world, the military, and other aspects of society as well. Corrupting the nation through education, the church, and society had begun. This devious attempt was the beginning of paving the way for other unforeseen actions in the future.

AFTERMATH OF SENSITIVITY TRAINING THAT INFILTRATED AREAS FOR SUPPORT

Sexual Revolution

This was one of the goals of sensitivity training (communist method to infiltrate from within) to remove inhibitions and smashed self-dignity, self-control, discipline, holy purity, and tear apart marriage vows taken before God Almighty. Its grooming was well carried out as planned. As a support of this effort, cable TV strongly came into play in the 1970s. Along this time period, in the latter 60s, 70s, and 80s, pornography freely entered the sanctity of every home, religious or non-religious that had cable TV. The desensitizing of holy purity and responsibility regarding sex was promoted with the freedom of sexual acts in movies and other areas to all ages and all genders. Free sex was seen as being in style.

Some of my middle school aged students were bragging about what they were allowed to watch on TV.

The flood gates to fornication, free sex, and adultery flew wide-open and tore apart those living in purity and marriages. Divorces increased tremendously and became common till it became safer to co-live first over entering into Holy Matrimony. This left children to try to survive without the close support of having both parents with them. Children were now divided between parents, some never to see them again along with other vices that entered their lives. Control of humans as a goal would be attained by the government with no values taught or guidance given to children by their parents.

When teaching at the elementary level during the explosion of divorces throughout the nation, my third graders had such a difficult time dealing with their parents breaking up. A few started to have bed-wetting problems at night. Some others had their world crushed and flattened by the lack of morals, integrity, and selfishness by the adults in their lives. One could see them with blank faces, or tears rolling down their cheeks as they waited to line up to return home when school was dismissed. One student would loiter around the classroom just to remain out of the house a little longer.

When I moved to teach high school, my students in homes that were being broken in divorce would just act out with anger but the hurt within their hearts was seen through their eyes.

The rapid rate of homosexuality, adultery, and child sexual abuse increased even among the clergy and religious. Monasteries and rectories were also not spared. By the 80s, the church was laden with so much sex abuse against adults, teens, and children. All of this was followed up with cover-ups within the church itself.

Again, the warning of the third secret of Fatima was not heeded.

Psychology and its misuse

At this time, around the 1980s, the misuse of Maslow and Erickson's psychology moved into the forefront of education and seeped also into many denominations of different ministries and churches. Taking care of the basic human needs such as food, security, belonging, etc. are fundamental bodily and emotional needs for every human being, but the spirit of the human soul was somewhat forgotten by the churches or shoved into the background of humanity. In addition, the Self-Identity, Me, Myself, and I are important in self-concept and identity, but not at the expense of others due to one's selfishness and lack of respect for thy neighbor.

Values Clarification – Its misuse resulted in relativism

And then clinical studies such as values clarification, besides encounters, and sensitivity training that should have been kept at the clinical level, entered public and religious institutions, schools as well as churches, businesses, and every aspect of life. One could not teach students what choice to make. It was up to the student to decide, such as, to take drugs or not.

Teaching now at a religious high school in the early 1980s, a brother in a religious order stated that he no longer quotes the Bible or talks about sin. Let the students see for themselves, and make their own choices. Another department chair stated and shared the same venue that the kids need to make their own choices for their behaviors. We are not to tell them what is right or what is wrong; do not influence them, only if they ask. Values are now relative to their thinking. This was the result of following the values clarification method meant only for clinical treatments. Let students decide for themselves. This then seeped into the home and families lessening the rights of parents over their children. Whose goal was this?

Too often, educators of public as well as private and religious schools follow trends and fads, especially those that connect to the learnings of an individual, without sufficient thought, and use them, even if it is implemented on the wrong level. At that time, a few educators and religious leaders, but not all, and myself, felt that if students are not taught values, beginning with universal ones such as goodness, respect, etc., and if we do not try to live out values as examples to them, how then can they make good, sound decisions as they struggle to deal with and live out the moral and immoral arrows shot at them throughout their lives.

Have you noticed how the changes have followed the forces set in motion in the early years by the Freemasons, Marxists, and Communists? Annihilate from Within.

By this time, it was most difficult to find any priest that was well learned in spiritual experiences. But with prayers, I continued onward.

PRAYER TO THE MOTHER OF GOD

As more humanistic and progressivism continued in the aftermath of Vatican II, another brother from a religious order in the early 1980s mentioned that it is ok to just pray the second part of the Hail Mary prayer. I thought it odd that he would say that as the first part clearly calls upon the Immaculate Mary as the mother of God without any falsehood or doubt. It further confirms that JESUS CHRIST came in the flesh. Here are a few ideas.

Note: **Hail Mary**, full of grace (Her Immaculate Conception, no stain of sin)

The Lord is with Thee (appointed by God the Father)

Blessed are You amongst women (equity of all humans)

And Blessed is the Fruit of Thy Womb (Jesus Christ has come in the flesh, born of a virgin Mary)

Holy Mary, Mother of God (Trinity of the Father, Son (JESUS), and as the spouse of the Holy Spirit)

Pray for us sinners (help us on earth, destroy all evil as we battle with the 7 capital sins)

Now and at the hour of our death (be with us at the threshold as we enter our new life with God)

Amen (so be it done with heavenly peace)

The warnings of the third secret from the Mother of God, Our Lady of Fatima which should have been revealed in 1960 before Vatican II, were still being held in secret at this time. And the search for spiritual guidance continued, by others as well.

Drug Addictions

This was coupled with drug use, from marijuana to date drugs, cocaine, opioids, especially ice (crystal methane), that took the conscience of a person and twisted it around so that what was holy was seen as evil, and what was evil was seen as holy.

Subliminal Music

If a teacher warned a student about highly suggestive immoral actions or words of vulgarity in the music, students who were addicted to the loudness, rhythm, and beat of such music could not see any danger at all. "But it's the in-thing sir," would be a common response given to me from my students.

Games-Dungeons and Dragons, Ouija Boards/cloths, Seances, Psychics, Paranormal Activities, Books, Toys, Clothing.

These areas were practiced before but became so popular in the 70s and 80s.

Games: such as Dungeons and Dragons captured the minds and emotions of some young people, teens, and adults into the environment of the game and its mind control trigger. However, due to the lack of playing the game properly, violent behaviors resulted in the person believing that he or she was doing what was right by transferring the behaviors contained in the game into their real life.

Some of the teachers would warn the students about taking the needed proper caution if parents allowed them to play such games and share them with their parents.

Ouija Boards are also imprinted on cloths and wall hangings: this should never be played as it opens the doors/portals of other dimensions and allows any being to enter into your dimension. Only God has the right to allow other beings to enter, at His time, according to His Divine Will. If you, do it on your own, unknowingly, an evil one may enter and you will be subject to much suffering for you alone will have to deal with it.

Ironically, I came across a magazine that sold the Ouija board imprinted on a table cloth and as a wall hanging. In the other half of the magazine, medals of the Blessed Mother, Mary Immaculate, and of St. Benedict, known to dispel evil, were being sold also. Therefore, one must be very prudent today in what we come across.

> My parents personally knew of a case where a couple played the Ouija Board constantly. At night, in the corner of the ceiling in one of the rooms, an evil shadow took residence there from being called forth from the Ouija board game. They lived in fear, night after night until they could no longer stand it. They quickly sold the house and moved away.
>
> Perhaps because we all share earth; we need to leave the dimensions of lives on earth in their rightful areas or planes. For example, between the coffee table and myself, the space in between may be occupied by other souls. A book entitled Psychic Warrior by David Morehouse depicts his true experiences as a psychic person in dealing with such dimensions.

Seances, Psychics: In these areas, one must be prudent. If these people are truly gifted by God, and some certainly are, their gifts will be used to help and support others to carry their cross or crosses, and move towards God. It has been warned that if any God-given gifts are used only for self-notoriety or richness, they can be turned against a person, destroyed, or even removed.

Paranormal Activities: So popular in the late 90s and a score of the 20s. These shows appear so scientifically interesting. But again, when dealing with other dimensions, unless it is granted by God alone, one must beware. It has been stated that as a result of these shows, some or many of those involved in it seek spiritual help because of opening portals that should not have been opened. Again, the book, Hauntings, Possessions, And Exorcisms by Adam C. Blai are recommended in these areas.

Books: that promote curses, spells, and conjure evil spirits may appear as fantasy. However, many are actual words used by evil doers. As such, Catholic Schools in Tennessee, after consulting with exorcists in Rome and the United States, followed their recommendations and removed Harry Potter books from their shelves.

Star - Advertiser, Catholic school bans Harry Potter, p. A2, Associated Press, Tuesday 9-3-2019

Others: The same holds true with other children's toys or clothing, that have such attached to them. Chronic illness whenever playing or wearing such could be traced to origins containing curses and the like.

So how does a teacher educate his or her students who are being bombarded with all of these changes that are affecting their minds, self-concept, self-esteem, and their relationships with others, with no sound values or judgments to follow? There were many changes in student behaviors seen as time went on, even within the realm of parental duties.

One of my high school students remarked that they no longer had to follow elementary rules, that things have changed, and that they are free to do things like chew gum in class whenever they felt like it. Discipline began to disappear and make way for a free- for- all- attitude.

Many students were playing Dungeons and Dragons. Warnings to use it only as a game and to keep it outside of one's life were given to the students. Parents, who were so busy trying to make ends meet with one or two jobs daily, had to be educated in these areas that were taking hold of their children's lives.

With the sexual revolution and the coming out of the closet, another student asked me, "Mister John, would you hate me if I was to become a homosexual?" I responded to him, "Of course not! I may not agree with your behavior, but I would still respect you and love you as we should love our neighbor. You, yourself, know what God asks of you. The cross that you carry will be between you and God."

One could also see the changes that took hold of parents with parental rights, student rights, students with disability rights, and what have you. The relationships of parents to teachers, schools, and administrators were beginning to change with the lack of support for schools, teachers, and school administrators. They were overcome with me, myself and I, their rights from the federal government especially those with disabled children, rather than working collaboratively for the sake of their child. Exploiting the systems with lawsuits for monetary gain besides services needed, or even services that should have been performed by parents themselves and not thrown upon the schools also became popular in some areas. There was a point where much more federal and state funding was given to the small number of students with disabilities, while a large number of non-disabled students went without.

Black lightning bolts in the dark sky at midnight-Seeking help for spiritual guidance

By now, it was thought that life would now proceed normally. But on a Sunday night in February 1981, while driving home from a hospital close to midnight, I saw back lightning bolts streaking down from the top heights of heaven to earth. These were intense, jet-black bolts against the dark black of night. The bolts were so jet-black that they stood out against the total blackness of the night sky. The jet-black lightning bolts remained in a permanent stance for a while. Somehow, there was a sense that it was not a good sign. After testing myself to see if it was my imagination or not, looking away and then visually returning to it, rubbing my eyes, looking back and forth repeatedly, it was confirmed that it was truly happening. Bewildered and shaken, a call was made to a spiritual friend upon arrival at home.

He directed me quickly to the Holy Bible, LUKE 10:17-18.

"And the 70 returned with joy, saying, Lord, even the demons are subjected unto us by the use of thy name. At that he said to them, I began to behold Satan already fallen like lightning from heaven. Look! I have given you the authority to trample underfoot serpents and scorpions, and over all the power of the enemy, and nothing will by any means do you hurt. Nevertheless, do not rejoice over this, that the spirits are made subject to you, but rejoice because your names have been inscribed in the heavens." Warfare!

Within a few days later, another friend shared that he saw the jet-black bolts of lightning in the dark sky also, that did not move like normal bolts of lightning do. He, too, searched for its meaning in the Bible. It confirmed what was seen and experienced.

DEALING WITH CHANGES WITHIN THE CATHOLIC CHURCH

Change of Habits-wear:

St. Padre Pio, who died in 1968, and had the gift of bi-location, the stigmata, and insight of reading into people, stepped outside of the confessional and approached a man wearing an ordinary shirt. Padre Pio instilled in him the sanctity of his Ordained Ministry and to dress at all times as a priest. This is in reverence to God and his consecration to God. It is also a sign of sacrifice, to live in poverty, obedience, and chastity. One should read the book, "Padre Pio, The Stigmatist", by Rev. Charles Mortimer Carty. Tan Books and Publisher, INC., Rockford, Illinois 61105, in the year 1989.

A friend of mine shared how things looked different. He sat next to a nun who left the traditional habit on the sideline and was now dressed as an ordinary woman. She showed him the beautiful gold earrings and chains around her neck. And she also shared how she goes weekly to the beauty shop to have her hair done. He felt uneasy as he barely made enough money to buy his wife even one gold necklace chain. His wife was lucky enough to have a haircut once every two months. Something of reality and the spiritual life seem off-balance in his mind.

Ecumenism, inculturation, acceptance of all religions:

Again, the lack of discernment from one extreme to another, keeping other religions apart, and now including all within without a profound explanation for unity.

Ideologies:

Gnosticism-like Luther, who promoted that faith without good works will grant you salvation, the Gnostics promoted that all you need is knowledge. What you do in life can be completely opposite to the knowledge that you obtain, and that does not matter, as long as you have knowledge. FC 118 Spring 2017 p. 32

Arian-Similarly, a government policy in the 4th century promoted an Arian heresy that Jesus Christ was not equal to the Father in divine nature, but just similar. FC 118 Spring 2017 p. 29

The equality among all of the diverse religions lies in the belief in one God. That is good. Among the differing denominations, there may be beliefs or non-beliefs in Jesus Christ, or even that Jesus is the Son of God, the Blessed Mother of God, the Trinity, etc. The profound insight into the Divinity of God lies in the Blessed Trinity as revealed in Sacred Scripture, especially in the teachings of the Son, Jesus Christ, and handed down through the Apostles. As such, the Catholic Church is the main line from which other churches may stem from. The lessening of their lines occurs when they begin to distance themselves from the twelve truths in the Apostle's Creed. Does that make sense to you, dear reader?

Situation Ethics:

Resulting in the reception of Holy Communion by the divorced and remarried, the use of contraception, the movement towards homosexuality, and other behaviors once forbidden by the ten commandments, especially the 6th, and 9th commandments produced confusion for some laity.

There is room for situation ethics, as long as the morality of the action is addressed and not just given up to natural laws. The situation surrounding it must be dealt with on the moral level as connected to the natural level to bring justice about.

My grandmother was divorced and never missed mass her whole life. Because she was divorced, she was not able to receive the Holy Eucharist physically. But she did receive the Holy Eucharist spiritually at every single mass that she attended till the day she died. She never missed her Sunday Masses. Should she have been allowed to receive the Holy Eucharist during her time?

The optional use of creeds, between the Apostle's Creed and the Nicene Creed:

This presents a great **danger** to the catholic religion as the Apostle's Creed contains all of the very basic truths of the religion. If the Trinity was of concern, Vatican II could have just added the term, "consubstantial" to the Apostle's Creed? The basic truths would still exist to guide the individual throughout life.

Example: "…and in Jesus Christ, His Son, Our Lord, consubstantial to the Father, suffered, died, and was buried…."

St. Thomas Aquinas -Doctor of the Church, as noted in The Fatima Crusader 115 p 9, 2016, points out the importance of each of the twelve articles in the Apostle's Creed as showing the soul the pathway to God in heaven.

Some physical changes:

The re-arrangement of the pews and alters now facing the congregation and the disappearance of statues in some churches. Some removed the statues in agreeing with the accusations from others that parishioners were worshipping them and not God. They failed to see that the statues are the same as having pictures of their loved ones at home, as reminders of love and devotion, and nothing else.

Spiritual and devotional works of art were replaced with modern art, which displayed more of the modern world of the beauty of lines, intersections, curves, and heights, leaving spiritual values on the wayside.

Because of all the changes occurring, in 1984, the urge to write again was strong and so another attempt was made to help souls to deal with spiritual experiences from what I learnt from others as I found it so difficult to find the necessary guidance needed. The writing also included how the church was changing. The writing was presented with full trust to a Bishop. Hoping to have open conversations with him, he did not agree nor would accept it. But he was willing to meet with me. It ended there as I knew it was at a standstill.

More incidences occurred, and more learnings from God.

Out-of-body experience that happens to many people

> In the very early morning hours of the mid-80s, while asleep next to my spouse, I felt and saw my being travel through a dark tunnel towards a bright illuminated light as if it was moving towards and through my head. This was followed by a deep sense that I was out of my body. Thinking of a close friend who lived on a distant island, within an instant, I was there in his home. No time went by, no distance was traveled. Yet somehow, there was a strong sense that it was 5:00 am. I heard and knew that my friend's daughter entered the house. Although I could not physically see them, I was spiritually there and heard both of them greet each other. Remembering that my spouse was sleeping beside me, the need to get back to the side

of my spouse seemed necessary. Again, in an instant, I found myself entering my body through the bright illuminated light and then the dark tunnel. Sleep continued. Awakening at 9:00 am, I called my friend immediately and asked if his daughter came at 5:00 am at home and shared how they greeted each other. He was surprised that I knew of the visit. It was confirmed that it did happen!

WHAT IS DEATH LIKE?

It appeared that with death, there is no time or distance to travel in the next world except when we leave our earthly bodies. And we do still live in a pure soul-spirit state of being. There is no end to life, just to the body. In the Bible Jesus also states, "In the resurrection, neither do men marry nor are women given in marriage but are as angels in heaven." Matthew 22:30

Others may be able to share more with you, dear reader. Each out-of-the-body experience is so unique and learnings from such awakenings are so individualized. How God created each one of us is very beautiful.

An Awakening by the public school system:

In 1987, employment was then in the public school system. And by 1989, it was evident to many, that America was becoming a cesspool for the negative aspects of life. It took the public school system in a state, and not the church, to take the lead to bring back character education into the life of the students. The teaching of values through guidance counseling, student mediation, reflecting on what was right, what was wrong, and how to repair disrespect was welcomed by all.

Continuing in education, in 2003, a minister from a protestant denomination approached me one afternoon as I was leaving the school grounds. He warned me about being careful regarding which church would use our school facilities. He had written a pamphlet on being on the lookout for churches who sexually abuse parishioners, adults, children, and other clerics and how there was so much cover-up taking place in the Catholic Church.

Little heed was paid to it but there was an awakening of its happenings in all aspects of life, in churches, businesses, medicine, military, families, clubs, organizations, whatever else there is. Moreover, many Catholics left or just parted from the church with all of the upheavals that were occurring. And sadly, vocations to the priesthood, brotherhood, and convent nuns decreased.

Unexpectedly, in 2020, a document consisting of V volumes, written in 2012, "the Rite of Sodomy," by a top investigative reporter, Randy Engel, New Engel Publishing, Export Pennsylvania, was sent to me by a religious organization. It listed many clerics, including the Bishop whom I had shared my writing with, and who evidently denied what was written regarding the changes taking place within the church, as a perpetrator of homosexuality. Another local report on "Survivors of Sexual Abuse" stated how his diocese was open wide to the world and invited many sexually abusive clerics. Many responded to his invitation.

It also mentioned the death of a 13-year-old altar boy and many other cases of abuse that the church so manipulatively covered up. Rite of Sodomy, Vol III p. 683.

With reflection, it was God's way of saying that there is much to learn. As someone pointed out, never give up. Jesus Christ fell 3 times; He never gave up. Even to the end, He never gave up, only His Spirit to God.

Voices calling your name, do not respond

These are common occurrences with many individuals. Sometimes it happens when a person is awake, or when a person is just about awakening from sleep, but not fully awake, more of being semi-awakened. Some cultures will respond, while others follow the warfare protection of **do not respond, as you do not know the origin and intent of the sender.** Tricks are being played upon you by demons. Do not open the portal.

Just ignore it and with prayer, leave it in God's hands.

Such experiences occurred. Once with a voice, I could not identify with. This was left in God's hands. Two other times, it was the voice of my spouse who was in the hospital. I responded automatically upon awakening and phoned my spouse to see if there was any matter to tend to. Since there was none, and my spouse directly stated that she did not call me at all, it was just avoided with prayer, and handled, in the same manner, the second time.

When there is no proper response to Did Jesus Christ come in the flesh, avoid it. Rebuke it in the holy name of Jesus Christ. In some situations, it was shared that no anger is needed at times. Just send it back to where it belongs in Jesus' name.

If there is a positive response, yes, Jesus Christ has come in the flesh, and still, there is an uneasy feeling, send it back to where it belongs stating that prayers will be offered for it. Others who know how to deal with such firsthand may be able to write a book to help everyone.

One culture emphatically tells its people that it is important to not respond, just walk away, especially if walking by a cemetery. Something not of good nature or evil may or will come about.

Beware of the following: others who do respond by opening the portal to voices heard or through **mental telepathy** thinking that they are being gifted by God, end up being controlled by its fraud ant source. Its intent is to lead the person away from God and rob the person of his or her energies of the mind, spirit, emotions, and body and ultimately destroy the soul.

Let God alone show you what is being communicated to you. He will do so not according to your time, but in His own time when it is right for you. **Pray.**

Sacramentals

The use of sacramentals helps many souls in warfare. Crucifixes, medals of Jesus, Mary, the Trinity, Saints, Holy Water, Printed Prayers, Statues of Jesus, Mary, Saints, Angels, Rosaries, Blessed palms, scapulars, and any holy and blessed item that moves the soul to God for help and protection.

During a long time period, over twenty years ago, a crucifix that faced upward with our Lord during the daytime would sometimes be found turned over the next morning upon awakening. This continued for about 6 months. I did wonder if someone in the household was doing this. It has not been settled yet but there is a rightful suspect.

Just recently, a book entitled: Hauntings, Possessions, And Exorcisms by Adam C. Blai, was looked into. It verified much of what I had learnt orally through conversations with several spiritual people as to how demons play tricks and move things, like sacramentals. One just needs to rebuke such in Jesus 'name. Also, always ask God for His Divine Protection for yourself and your loved ones when dealing with negative forces.

Destroying Negativity in Objects: Pictures

In the 1990s, a framed picture of a lovely hula maiden, drawn with beautiful colors using the medium of color chalks/pastels, hung on a wall in the living room. Many times, her face appeared beautiful, at other times... stern, especially her eyes. It was thought that it could be due to one's imagination, a simple explanation.

One day, a minister came to bless the house. He was gifted by the Most High to see beyond the walls and doors. As he passed a closet with its doors closed, he mentioned that there was a wooden bowl on the floor within. He stated that it should not remain empty and to put something in it. As he passed the picture of the maiden, he asked that it be removed and placed on the floor facing an altar of Jesus Christ in the home. He continued to bless the house as I was in a state of wonderment as to why he requested such.

After partaking in a light lunch, he asked that I pick up the framed picture and take a look at it. Lo and behold, when the framed picture was turned around, the entire picture had a blackish hue with the eyes of the maiden circled in black sneering, emitting anger and hate! Gone was the beautiful maiden. The deep realization overcame me that it was not due to imagination but to something not good.

Immediately, the minister said that he would take it and destroy the evil with fire. Evidently, fire is the medium that will destroy such. This picture came about due to a strong relationship between the artist and the subject. Because it was bought as a gift for a family member, I replied that it would be better to have it returned to him and convey what had happened.

Since culture overtook the spirit, it was consequently to be torn up and discarded in the trash bin. As I opened the glass wooden frame, the entire picture instantly crumbled to complete fine dust, a little blown by the wind, and the rest discarded in the trash bin along with its expensive wooden frame. Prayer was offered up to remove it entirely from our midst.

Immaculate Heart of Mary Overcomes Evil

Evil aspects of culture affect even the innocent people. Within some cultures, unchristian people called upon negative spirits to do evil to others. These negative spirits from the dead may appear as fireballs.

Long ago, a woman close to me experienced such. One evening when walking home, she saw a fireball flying through the air, aiming at the basement of her house. These were known as lost souls controlled by the living with evil intentions, such as placing curses. Her culture dealt with such by swearing at it. But because she was close to the Mother of God, Mary Immaculate, she called upon The Mother of Jesus Christ, and the fireball burst.

Cemetery

Many people have experienced regarding souls at cemeteries but hold back in sharing with others due to fear of being seen as crazy and the like. No, you are not crazy. Prayer is important. Here are three true experiences of such.

1. Barbara was a highly spiritual person and was allotted with God's ministry on earth in a very unique way. She was able to help souls to God when they were released to meet with her

in the wee hours at a cemetery. Actual conversations occurred between her and souls that she could actually see, and guidance was given to the souls to reach out to God, through Jesus Christ. Souls who were lost, of all ages, even those of children, would be in contact with her in order for her to guide them to our Heavenly Father. Prayers were offered, and of course, the rosary was prayed daily.

On one occasion at the cemetery following a funeral, she remarked to me that she smelled a stench of a soul in a grave as we passed by when walking to the designated plot for the recently deceased. She asked if I sensed it also. I responded that I did not, yet knowing that she would have something to settle about it with God Almighty.

2. Brenda was an ordinary Christian that often visited her family's burial sites to put flowers there and say a few prayers. On one occasion when she returned to her car to return home, she heard a bump in the back seat of the car just as she drove away from the cemetery. The back window of the car was opened. As she looked at the rear mirror, she sensed and somewhat saw a presence and began to pray. When arriving home, she rebuked it in Jesus' name and sent the spirit back assuring prayers in the event it needed such.

3. Mary was a loving person who would also visit family plots to lay flowers and offer prayers. After a visit, whenever she would sleep and fail to awaken at the right time for work, her bed would shake to awaken her. This happened very often if she was late to awaken. After discussing it with a minister, she was prayed over and the shaking stopped. The caring soul was put to rest and free to travel to where God wanted it to go.

Help from Heaven through a Relative

Aunty Tina, in 1978 at the age of 80, shared an experience of a time when she was much younger and so deathly ill, that the doctors did not know how to treat her. As she lay suffering in illness on her bed at home, her sister, who had died earlier appeared to her in a natural human form and dress attire. She told her what to drink, an extremely saturated solution. After forcing the drink down her throat, she started to vomit at certain intervals. Within a short time, she felt well and went back to see the doctor. She was cured to the doctor's amazement!

Schizophrenia vs. Other and the importance of God in One's Life

It is important to know the difference between mental illnesses and possessions.

There was an instance when I witnessed a person, with a firm belief in God Almighty and Jesus Christ, swaying from side to side uncontrollably. She appeared weakened with the mumbling of words that it was difficult to understand what was being said. She was also unable to stop the movements of her legs.

As soon as it was mentioned that she would be taken to see the doctor, immediately she stopped the movements of her legs and spoke in a very clear voice and not mumbling, stating that she was fine and nothing was wrong with her. A complete change of personality and physical movements occurred.

She then walked away calmly, in full control of her being. She does suffer from schizophrenia.

It was told that some people suffering from schizophrenia are just extremely auditorily sensitive to sound that they are able to pick up the sound even from a neighbor's house.

Lost, and Help from Heaven was Sent

This is about a mother and her daughter, Sarah, at the age of 10, who had just moved to a new state to live along with the rest of the family. Everything was new to them, the streets, shops, medical buildings, and the like. One day when running errands, the mother and daughter Sarah, got totally lost. They kept driving around and around looking for their destination. Feeling a little frightened, with no one around to help them, they did not know what to do. Now to find their way home. Suddenly, out of the blue, two Asian men appeared to them. They were neatly dressed in black suits, around the ages of 30, and smiling. One had glasses on. Being taken back for fear of strangers, her mother wanted to protect Sarah. The men in a very helpful tone of voice simply told her to, "backup and go that way," as if they knew she was lost. "Go that way," they repeated.

The mother backed up and went in the direction they pointed to. And they arrived at their destination. After completing the most important errand, they drove back to look for the men to thank them and there was absolutely no one in sight. It was a large open area where no one could hide. And the errand was very short allowing sufficient time for the mother and Sarah to return to thank the men.

At the age of 27, Sarah was looking through family pictures sent to them by a relative. When she came across a picture of her great grandfather and his friend, she yelled out to her mother that those were the men who helped them. Mother looked at the pictures and agreed that it was her grandfather with his glasses on at a younger age and his friend who was sent from heaven as angels to help them. God is kind and loving.

Aura

Some people are gifted with being able to see the aura or light emitting from people or any living beings. Lynn, a gentle and good soul, is able to see the aura of people as if in a protective bubble. She is also able to detect if anyone is ill just by being in their presence.

One day, while standing in a checkout line at a supermarket, she saw the aura of the person next to her in line and told her that she was not well and to see a doctor. The person responded that she was thinking of doing so and now will certainly do it.

Some of us are able to see the aura of people. The aura of a teacher that was shown to me one day in the school office was so striking. It was a bright glow around the entire person, a very bright white light. This person was a strong advocate for doing what was just, and fair, and executed what was right with goodness in all dealings with other people. I have never seen this aura on such a scale again.

Gems and Feathers from Heaven

Joyce was a very sincere warm person and a Christian who wished others the best. She had always heard about the falling of gems and feathers from heaven from other Christians who did truly experience such. Returning excitedly in the mid-2000, from a travel to the Holy Land, she blurted out the blessed experience of actually being there as gems and feathers fell upon her and the group of other Christians that she was with. Hesitantly and yet with a sense of humor, she was asked if she was certain that there were no birds flying over, to which she scolded me and stated, "No, it really happened! It is feathers from angel wings!"

Pulsating Sun Beams in The Sky

In 2021, on a clear mid-morning sunny day at the beach, as I sat upon a rock surrounded by the gentle sea water looking up at the sky, I was captured by what was seen. The beautiful yellow/ white sun-beam rays penetrated through the white clouds in the sky. I thought to myself, wow, what a beautiful sight of nature to see. Then, it happened. The sun beams started to pulsate like the beating and pulsating of the human heart. I could not believe what was being seen and was taken back with much uneasiness. Refusing to continue to look up, a friend by the name of Joe was texted as to what was seen. He shared that it was what is called cosmic energy or a circadian rhythm that pulsates with all the energies within the cosmic realm. God's balancing of His Creation.

After much ponderance and searching, the realization of the balance in God's creation with the movements of the planets and moons, their internal magnetic fields, gravitational and centrifugal forces, stars and the traveling of sound and light waves, cosmic explosions, dark holes, the solar waves of the sun, all with the receiving movements from the surfaces of all planets and asteroids, so much more, must be held in some common movement to prevent it from falling in all directions and into total destructive chaos.

Our Great Creator God Almighty, is holding all in balance by His Almighty Power. It is we, or other creatures that we are unaware of, that will set things off balance. Look at how bombs are sent to the center of the earth by humankind. How do we send satellites into space and leave the rubbish floating around. Other actions can set off the balance. Comparable is climate change that is hitting earth due to what earthlings have done to themselves with its carbon emission, controlling the weather, and using the electromagnetic field as a source for physical warfare. Some results are extreme and devastating earthquakes, floods, drought, fires, and shortages of food and medicine. Many more calamities will be seen such as new diseases.

I then thought, ok, God, more learnings in the area of science that comes from you, alone. Presently, there is an awareness that God continues to teach all of us, including you, dear readers. At this time more books are being published and are being made available regarding spiritual guidance for souls. Thanks be to God!

Visitations of evil and the Power of The Holy Name of Jesus Christ

Sam at a very young age got into a car accident and faced death. His skull was fractured and other parts of his body were severely damaged. Upon awakening from that day on, he would be in terrible pain. It was common to think that he would not make it at all. But the Good Lord had plans for him. Sam survived. After being born into the church at age 21, around the age of mid-twenties, Sam started to have frightening visitations. When sleeping and lying in the dark room, upon awakening, he would see a dark presence floating around his room. With great fright, which also froze and kept his mouth closed, he would cast the spirit out in the Holy Name of Jesus Christ with the strength of his spirit. After going through this two times, it stopped completely.

Like many who face death at a young age and are faced with evil warfare and learn to reach out to Jesus Christ, there seems to be a pull towards wanting to help others, as good Samaritans, especially in the field of medicine or a similar profession. Just sharing an opinion.

Welcoming into Heaven by Angels

Solomon's mother-in-law lay dying in her bed. The family knew that time was near and kept in daily prayer. His wife and others would check in on her frequently. In the final moments, his wife decided to remain in the room. It was a very still day, with no wind whatsoever. When it was God's time, his wife saw a beautiful smile on her mother's face. In a graceful moment of time, the curtains of the bedroom window moved slowly, with no wind around. Then they fluttered open, and then, gracefully closed. Again, no wind was there. The presence of angels was felt. The family attests that the mother's soul was taken to the Lord by angels. So much peace followed.

This spiritual experience inaugurated an initial movement to research angels.

ANGELS

There are many books out there on angels. The connection between their existence to cosmic beings is seen in books in this age today.

Common knowledge about angels are:

- that they are spiritual beings or incorporeal

- that they consist of 9 choirs.

- that the Archangels Michael guards the North, Uriel the East, Gabriel the South, and Raphael the West

- In 1950, Poe Pius XII attributed St. Michael the Archangel to be the patron of all Police Officers.

- It is also known that Pope Leo the XIII after a vision of war and suffering allowing evil to run wild for a century, composed **the prayer to St. Michael the Archangel** to be said after Mass to defend us against all evil.

Saint Michael the Archangel, defend us in battle!

Be our protection against the wickedness and snares of the devil.

May God rebuke him, we humbly pray;

And do thou, O Prince of the heavenly host,

By the power of God,

Thrust into hell Satan and all the evil spirits.

Who roam through the world seeking the ruin of souls.

Unfortunately, this prayer was removed with Vatican II, allowing evil to run rampant globally until humankind turned toward peace and love towards the Higher Power. We need to remember that God's time differs from ours.

There are also evil angels (devils) and demons (humans) out to destroy the souls of humans. These need to be rebuked immediately in the Name of Jesus Christ.

Following are the nine choirs of the holy angels. Mary Immaculate is the Queen of the Holy angels.

1. **Seraphim**
2. **Cherubim**
3. **Thrones**
4. **Dominations**
5. **Virtues**
6. **Powers**
7. **Principalities**
8. **Archangels**
9. **Angels**

As previously stated, there may be doubt, hesitation, and lack of understanding from those who never had specific experiences as others on certain topics. Thus, even in dealing with angels, there is much complexity and sometimes confusion on the topic. Disagreements also occurred among St. Ambrose, St, Jerome, St. Thomas Aquinas, and even St. Paul. Dionysius and Thomas Aquinas seem to be more in agreement in the hierarchy of angels.

CLOSING PART II

By 2011, A Steep Climb by J.M. Joseph was written and completed after living it for more than 40 years. The reaction by some people who experience the walk in their lives wanted to have more written on it. So, it was then, in the year of 2017 that this second book was initiated. And again, to be able to help other souls.

By now, in 2022, more books are being published on spiritual experiences and how to deal with such. That is good. However, one must use discretion as to what to agree upon and disagree upon, as with this book as well. Faith in God, prayer, and guidance by the Holy Spirit will help one to discern the value and good in their readings and learnings.

The good news is that more ministers of God, Priests, and others, are now being trained in such. We all need to fight this warfare on earth. Together, we can move towards Peace on Earth.

This book will end with the learnings that were shared by many, many good people, laypeople, ministers from other denominations, priests, nuns, and others whom the Lord God allowed to put it all together. The following and last portion is from J.M. Joseph's book, A Steep Climb, Between Heaven and Hell, Writers' Branding, relaunched in 2021.

PEACE BE UNTO YOU.

Writings

To Lou, The Veteran

from John, The Eccentric

ON SPIRITUAL CONFRONTATIONS

From my **1973** writing:

ONESELF

A taste of the supernatural is indeed pleasant, or it can be of a revolting nature. When it is so pleasant, it can mislead one easily into "ego adoring ego" until it blinds itself and no longer sees its Creator, Our Heavenly Father. Evil is indeed cunning particularly when one tries with all sincerity to serve God, thus the importance and need of a Spiritual Director. Such neglect could result inevitably in the service to oneself, eventually to self-destruction through prolonged states of soul tormentation in discerning the meanings of spiritual confrontations, being preoccupied with WHY? WHAT TO DO? HOW? When it is so revolting, fear of the unknown and stages of depression may set in and increase with depth as time lingers on, self pity. In addition, if the experience granted is of the "awful," a fear far beyond the natural realm must be coped with.

ON SPIRITUAL CONFRONTATIONS

From my **1989** writing up to the present. Lou, I omitted my 1984 writing.

What is the nature of these confrontations? How does one deal with them, or distinguish true ones from false ones?

As a minister recently shared with me, in dealing with God's realm on earth, we all have a role to play. Like on the battle field in war, some of us, as spiritual warriors, are front –line warrior fighters, some are fighters in tanks, ready to move in, some are in the air, on the waters, some are doctors, nurses, others are psychologists, and healers. Then there are those who do the strategic planning, while others are coordinators, cooks, those that dispense linen, clothes, artillery and guards. And there are many other roles. But whichever role you play, keep steadfast as a soldier of the Lord, without any fear.

We must rely on the Lord, Jesus Christ, to show us the way.

SPIRITUAL CONFRONTATIONS MAY OCCUR IN DIFFERENT STATES:

1. **Full Consciousness** – having control of all the faculties of the mind, reasoning, perception, memory, freedom of choice, etc.

2. **Semi – Consciousness** – having control of all the faculties of the mind as above; however, the body remains in an inert state like on the threshold between deep sleep and full awake ness.

3. **Unconsciousness** – asleep in a dream state. It is said that we should not believe in dreams. However, visions in dreams are of another nature. Use discernment here.

SPIRITUAL CONFRONTATIONS MAY OCCUR IN DIFFERENT FORMS:

1. **Meditations or Contemplations** – Self- voidance of oneself to be able to unite with the Divine Will. Least amount of distractions, the better. All people who meditate are aware of this. Many saints experience this to the highest degree.

2. **Visions** – These may leave a person in awe or in fear depending on its source. Visions may appear in regular hues of color to the illumination of bright white, gold white and blue white.

   The whiter in illumination it is, the higher in spirituality does the entity or source exists.

People who have shared their visions with me have stated that their visions have occurred through sight-supernatural, angelic, or preternatural-a departed one, some with sound, as talking to someone, and some with touch, feeling the other entity touch them. The latter examples start to move into the area of visitations.

A woman told me of the passing of her mother. Just before her last breath, her mother had a big smile upon her face and then expired. Even though there was no wind that day, the curtains gently moved, fluttered, opened, and then closed.

This is similar to the writings of those who describe various mediums used by God:

A priest shared the following with me from a book that he read, "Mystical Theology," by Durrant, which listed 3 mediums:

a. strictly supernatural
b. divine touches-vibrations, nebula, flashes, wind
c. natural-sensible, corporal, bodily.

Having experienced such and hearing from others, I would describe such experiences as:

a. the supernatural level-above the natural realm.
b. movement of different energies- divine in origin, expressed in a somewhat natural manner at times, touches, wind, visible and non-visible.
c. the natural level-seen with and experienced through the bodily senses.
d. there could be a combination of levels, such as, non-visible yet the presence is heard or felt or both.

Visions may be seen through the senses or through the intellect. Sense vision may at times be deceiving. The rule of thumb (learned this from someone who lived it consistently) in determining the source of visions is if the resulting force thrusts the soul towards goodness and the glorification of God, then it is of a good source. Teresa of Avila gives more value to intellectual vision. "Intellectual vision is more of certitude, bringing greater interior benefits and effects to the soul in going about in peace and desiring to please God." (3) In other words, because of its understanding or somewhat of an understanding, there is more of a direction (spiritual thrust, yearning) to serving God.

It is important to inform the reader that even though good visions are from God, Almighty, never ask for them or desire to follow that path. That opens another path that the soul may not be able to handle. I have found that souls who are granted such will walk through hell to do the will of God. Same as Judas Iscariot did, to accomplish the Holy Will of The Father. Same as those who help other souls (for example, helping drug users on Ice towards healing) to find their way to God. You, too, will walk through hell. Only God knows how much an individual can handle, and He allows us to take certain paths. Yet, He is always there with us, no matter how many times we have to walk through hell.

St. Teresa of Avila warns us about such and expresses how we must be humble, and be on guard as one can easily be deceived. Even the desires of the imagination can lead into seeing or hearing what is really not there, or dreaming what is desired. Most of all, she states, **"the trials suffered by those to whom the Lord grants these favors to, are not few, but extraordinary and of many kinds."** Therefore, "the safest way is to want only what God Wants." (4)

3. **Visitations:** The visitation by a spirit, or specter, be it good or evil, can leave you in a state of dismay, or completely frozen. I remember hearing a statement of a person "being frozen to death." Fear is the weapon of the devil. When such fear occurs, just call upon the **Holy Name of JESUS**. All Bibles contain the Letter of St. John, Chapter 4. It states "Beloved, do not believe every spirit, but test the spirits to see whether they are from God: because many false prophets have gone out into the world. By this you know the spirit of God: **every spirit that confesses that Jesus Christ had come in the flesh is from God." 1 John 4:1-2**

Because evil is cunning, this question will force it to reveal itself. Evil is so undermining that it can appear as a holy angel or even quote the Bible. So, test all spirits, and rebuke them in the Holy name of Jesus Christ who has come in the flesh if it is of an evil source.

God allows Visitations for the following reasons:

a. It is allowed out of love-a visit from a loved one.
b. A message is to be given. I met an elderly person who shared with me that when she was severely ill, her departed relative (who appeared in regular human form with regular clothes) visited her and told her exactly what to do to get well. She followed her relative's instructions and after a few days was totally recovered.
c. The soul or spirit wants help and is in need of prayers. Only the living can help the dead, with prayer. As prayer is received by God, the soul is helped and its appearance becomes normal and is seen to be happy. The Holy Sacrifice of the Mass is the highest form of help to a soul. This is the greatest solace and support to all souls, especially for the souls of those who committed suicide.

Therefore, shouldn't all the living be praying for the dead who want spiritual help to move towards God? And, as they get closer to God, they (souls of light), in turn, can ask the Almighty to help us, the living, on earth.

Visitations and visions can occur simultaneously.

4. **Bi-location**: Padre Pio, as seen in the following book, "Padre Pio- The Stigmatist," by Carty, had this gift among others. And as all gifts should be used, he used them to glorify God by helping souls. Bi-location, being in two places at one time, covers no distance or time as it exists in the present. It is the separation of the spirit from the body, yet remaining in a total state of existence as one entity. A gift beyond the natural can destroy a person if it is not used to help a soul towards God.

5. **Voices: sensible sound.** Again, as in other confrontations, there is calmness yet, urgency. Leave it in God's Hands. He will show you what to make of it. Remember John, the Apostle, on how to test all souls.

WHY TEST THE SPIRITS?

According to St. John of The Cross, for every good spiritual confrontation, God will permit an evil one. This is for the soul's struggle to overcome obstacles and become strengthened. (5)

Once again, for every good vision, one must walk through hell. Hence, do not wish or want for a vision. Let it be God's Will. As a reminder, St. John's Letter tells us to test all spirits, "Did Jesus Christ Come in the Flesh?" The spirit who admits that Jesus Christ has come in the Flesh is of God. And if no acknowledgement in any form is given, rebuke it in the Holy Name of Jesus Christ. How then do we know that something other than good exists?

HELL

St. Teresa of Avila describes hell, "long and narrow alleyway, low dark and confined, foul stench and swarming with putrid vermin. It is the soul itself that tears itself to pieces…that interior fire and despair, in addition to extreme torments and pains… without end, never ceasing." (6) I met a friend who could stand in a cemetery at certain times, and point out graves whose souls smelled of stench. These souls would be helped to God if it was God's Will. Some people are gifted and guided by God to carry out this mission while on earth.

This also reminded me of many readings long ago, and of people sharing with me, that they believe that hell is here on earth. There are all the 7 capital sins bloated in humans, and when death comes, there is the grave, a hole in the ground. And the letter of St. John would always bring it to light that Jesus the Christ has come in the Flesh to open the gates of Hell. There is no Hell with Jesus, the Son of our Heavenly Father.

The three children at Fatima also give an account of hell. When our Lady stretched out Her Hands, "All at once the ground vanished, and the children found themselves standing on the brink of a sea of fire….. the terrified youngsters saw huge numbers of devils and damned souls. The devils resembled hideous black animals, each filling the air with despairing shrieks. The damned souls were in their human bodies and seemed to be brown in color, tumbling about… in the flames and screaming with terror. All were on fire within and without their bodies...neither devils nor damned souls seemed able to control their movements...There was never an instant's peace or freedom from pain." Our Lady mentioned that more souls are in hell due to the sins of the flesh. Prayers were and are asked for the souls in hell. (7)

Both accounts are very similar in description. And in Fatima's message, two entities are mentioned, the devils and demons.

HOW CAN THE PRESENCE OF EVIL BE DETECTED?

Identifying marks of evil spirits are:

1. When **no acknowledgement is given to** St. John the Young Apostle's question (to the living and the departed), "Did **Jesus Christ come in the Flesh?**" an atmosphere of ugliness is felt.

2. **Being trapped, distortion of goodness, and torment** are other aspects of negativity. A soul trapped in the **dark hole of self – pity**. Look for the light and move out; the sooner the better. Suicidal victims just needed a light to show them the way. Prayers, and most importantly, Holy Masses, would really help these souls, especially when they realize that can no longer solve the problems they had while on earth.

3. **Hot to Cold, or vice versa** – severe temperature changes within seconds. These changes could be physically felt or seen among humans through perceptions of the spirit, the intellect, or other.

4. **Stench, sulfur** – Its actual presence may be accompanied by the actual smell of sulfur, from the earth within. The senses can actually feel its presence, or circumstances of one's goodness can be twisted out of its state of goodness in secrecy by others. Psychology can be an excuse here.

5. **Fear** – may be accompanied with sensible sound; its actual presence is felt with uneasiness, ugliness, or fear itself. St. John of The Cross describes it as the soul is disturbed due to the presence of evil, horror seizes upon it. "This horrendous communication proceeds from

spirit to spirit manifestly and somewhat incorporeally …transcends all sensory pain. This spiritual suffering does not last long, for if it did the soul would depart from the body due to this violent communication. This experience remains in the soul's memory and causes great suffering." (8)

Hence the phrase, "frozen to death." It is truly a spirit-to-spirit confrontation. I would like to make it explicit that this type of confrontation is of an unearthly nature and so frightening that it can stop all involuntary functions of the body. Call upon Jesus immediately, with your mind/spirit.

What about fear as a result of inhumane treatment of others, such as threats, pressure, conniving, manipulation, jealousy, or a soul who succumbs to power in order to survive? This soul, no doubt, may lose its self- identity if the will, intellect, and soul give in entirely. Psychology and Psychiatry has its place here for human behaviors. For the spiritual aspects of individuals, psychology and psychiatry can join together to assist the forerunners of this area, the mystics, the ministers, the priests, the spiritualists, and reverends. There is a fine line between multiple-personalities and possession.

6. **Black Cloud or a black hue** – darkness of the mind (plurality of blaming), as well as a black shadow or even black lightning that may be seen by the human eyes. It is the opposite to the beauty of black. This is similar to negative white is the opposite to the beauty of white. Ancient prayers relate to deliverance from lightning. Over 40 years ago I came across a prayer asking God to free us from lightning and the damnation of hell.

Religious reasoning will direct the intellect to strengthen its faith in the Lord to handle what is about to occur. Faith does not have to be separated from the intellect, but rather, it can be its driving force.

On the human level, it is a stubborn atmosphere of blindness to the truth, and all expenditures of energy to bring the truth out is continuously blocked by a stubborn force. As a result, there is constant blaming of others due to the blindness, and the truth remains hidden. This could be seen in cultural pride, where suffering continues, church against church, etc. One must remember that there is always a common factor of truth to have an agreement upon, no matter how many disagreements may exist. This can bring about peace.

7. **Lack of dignity** – unbalanced within the mind and disheveled in appearance

8. **Noise: unrestful, loud; name calling:**
   A. Unnecessary loudness, thrashing behavior and the like emits from the individual. There is no calmness or peace. Note: there is a distinction between this type of behavior as opposed to mental illness.
   B. Name Calling, calling you by your name that can occur with the voice by a family member, or other. Refrain from responding, whether in an awakening stage from sleep, or even when passing a cemetery. You may ask Did Jesus Christ come in the Flesh? If uneasiness is felt, rebuke it in the name of Jesus Christ, send it back to where it belongs. Demons play tricks, to control and let you fall into evil.

9. **Abuse of drugs** – The abuses of drugs, especially, Ice/ Crystal Meth, are great in paralyzing the will with the sole purpose of preventing one in choosing good. Fear, whether through hallucinations, uncontrollable morbid thoughts, phobias, and voices etc. wipes out or turns the conscience inside out, so that good becomes evil and evil becomes good in the eyes of the soul. The mind becomes warped. Fear distorts the soul; it causes blindness of the soul. The abuse of drugs not only affects the body, but also the mind, the personality (psychology of a person), and the soul.

Research has also shown that the abuse of marijuana and alcohol has a tendency to release schizophrenia in individuals. What an easy pathway for crime to take place with such a combination and the lack of proper medical care. Further additional addictions along with the lack of medical assistance may result in dangers not only Healthwise but also spiritually.

One needs only to read the gospels of the Holy Bible to see many of these cases.

HOW TO GAIN STRENGTH IN DEALING WITH EVIL

EPHESIANS 6:10-17 "draw your strength from the Lord…Put on the armor of God…Our battle is not against human forces but against the principalities and powers, the rulers of this world of darkness, the evil spirits in regions above…put on the armor of God…truth as the belt around your waist, justice as your breastplate, and zeal to propagate the gospel of peace as your footgear…hold faith up before you as your shield; it will help you extinguish the fiery darts of the evil one. Take the helmet of salvation and the sword of the spirit, the word of God."

1. **The Holy Name of Jesus Christ** – rebuke evil only in His Holy Name. Command the demons/devils to go in the name of Jesus. In the Holy Name of Jesus Christ of Nazareth, I command you to leave immediately! Humans have absolutely no power of their own. Thus, the Holy name of Jesus Christ should always be revered and used in holiness and not in swearing or used lightly.

2. **The Crucifix** – Rebuke the evil spirit in the Holy Name of Jesus and hold the crucifix facing the direction of the presence of the ugly one. St. Teresa of Avila found that it must leave. The devils fear and tremble at the sight of a crucifix. However, should it be removed, they may return.

3. **Holy Water** – is always used by a priest when blessing a home. St. Teresa of Avila also found that Holy Water disperses evil spirits immediately and they never return. (9) Isn't this interesting, Lou?

4. **The Sign of The Cross** – as many Christians are aware of, it signifies the Blessed HOLY TRINITY, the Father, Son, and the Holy Spirit. We know that this is done with the actual movement of our hand, our praying out to God, and especially when a spirit confronts another spirit, our spirit calls out from the spiritual side of our soul. This is the same as calling out to Jesus Christ as previously stated. Someone shared with me how several people or more have used the sign of the cross to dispel evil. There is an account of a monk who made the Sign of the Cross over a youth whose features were distorted, and through the grace of God, was able to bring the features back

to normal. Now, Lou, I really don't know how distorted the features were, but it was written to be really bad!

5. **Stand Fast Against Fear** – We know through life experiences and psychology, that when the emotions take the lead, we are unable to think clearly and see the truth. Ask our Holy Mother, Mary Immaculate for help. Pray to St. Michael the Archangel to defend us in battle against the wickedness and snares of the devil, and by the power of God, cast the evil into hell etc. It has been said that the Holy Mother of Jesus Christ and St. Michael the Archangel battle evil.

   Stand fast with **Fortitude**, and do not give in to any fear. I call this stance as taking on holy anger. Be angry in holiness for God, and after facing it head on with holy anger, the evil must immediately leave. I have learnt this by articulating with other spiritual people and experiencing it myself.

   Have also learnt from reading a book by Ronald Knox, "An Autobiography of St. Theresa of Lisieux," that evil tries to make you subordinate to it through fear. It attempts to freeze you by stopping your flow of energy with God. As such, the emotions give in to fear, and your conscience is unable to function in connection with your intellect thereby severing your connection and ties with God. Fear then takes the lead. Anything to trick you into giving in to evil. Lou, this is what you were referring to.

6. **Words of Jesus – Luke 8:41-55** "Telita Cumi," Maid, arise. There are also other words that Christ used to dispel negativity. In a book by Sir E.A. Wallis Budge, entitled, "A History of Ethiopia-Nubia and Abyssinia, Vol. 1," Jesus Christ is depicted as confronting the evil eye and dispelling it with two words, "Asparaspes and Askoraskis."

   Lou, as you went through stages of healing due to your PTSD and alcoholism, souls with spiritual confrontations must do the same also. Faith and knowledge is so important. Like you, I, too, had to rely on the goodness of others to share their journeys, but on the spiritual realm. Let me share with you other ways of how souls can help themselves along their process of healing. Remember now, all that I share I learned from others whom God directed me to.

SELF-HELP FOR SOULS

1. **The Holy Sacrifice of the Mass** – especially the Holy Eucharist, the BODY and the BLOOD of OUR LORD, JESUS CHRIST (the price of LOVE that Jesus Christ paid to ransom us) is so sacred. Receive Our Lord daily, if possible. What strength there is in full possession of Jesus Christ, physically and spiritually. Remember, every time we receive Him, SINS ARE FORGIVEN, ours, as well as those for whom we pray, the living and the dead. Jesus promised this to us when He said to, "Do this in remembrance of Me" Luke 22:19. Masses help the living and the dead.

   Whenever a person dies, the Holy Sacrifice of the Mass is the greatest gift a living person can give to the deceased.

2. **Spiritual Nourishment – Prayer, Action, Readings**- As the body needs daily nourishment with food, so does the soul need daily nourishment with faith. Prayers, such Acts of Faith, Hope, and Charity, Spiritual and Corporeal Works of Mercy, Beatitudes Matthew 5:1-12, (faith without works is of no benefit), reading the HOLY SCRIPTURE, or BIBLE, reading materials on spiritual growth or self – growth, psychological reading as well, and stories on the Saints help provide nourishment for the soul.

3. **Devotions** – There are many patterns of prayers, some in litanies, novenas, Holy Hour-being in the true presence of the Lord, chaplet, to the Holy Trinity, devotions to the Sacred Heart of Jesus and the Immaculate Heart of Mary, the Rosary, and to the Saints and Angels. These increases one's relationship with God. They involve faith, action and especially, LOVE.

4. **Holy Objects – Sacramentals**: Let it be clear that one does not worship these objects. These are like having pictures of family members, reminders, representations of one's relationship to God the Most Powerful. Among these objects are the Rosary, statues, medals and holy pictures of Jesus, Mary, the Holy Trinity, Saints, Holy Angels, holy water, the Crucifix, blessed salt, the Scapular of Our Lady of Mount Carmel and more. When blessed, some of these have been used to rebuke evil immediately. Some have been

used in exorcism. Why? Because they represent God, the Father, the Son, and the Holy Spirit. And when blessed with Holy Water, is enveloped with God's Blessings. And evil is reminded through these objects that only God shall they worship.

5. **Conversations with others who are close to God and are willing to share their experiences**: I found so many people with much to share, so many who traveled the road like you and me, Christians helping Christians, ordinary men and women, ministers, religious, from all Christian denominations. As crazy as the conversations may sound to others who do not experience such, for those who are seeking God, such articulation is not so. Rather, these conversations enrich souls to move forward.

6. It is highly recommended that you, who are spiritual warriors/fighters, after reading the most important book, the **Bible**, read afterwards, books that are available such as the following: by **Ing, Richard, Spiritual Warfare**, Whitaker House, 1996. (10) It is a clear, dynamic book on how to handle evil situations and wars of spirituality. It even gives insights to the non-warriors.
Another book on deep spiritual warfare is one written by **Adam C. Blai, Hauntings, Possessions, And Exorcisms,** Emma us Road Publishing, 1468 Parkview Circle, Steubenville, Ohio 43953, 2017.

Unlike when this book, A Steep Climb by J.M. Joseph (incepted in 1973) was first copyrighted in 2011, there are now in 2022, other books that are being written regarding spiritual warfare.

In addition, this present book, J.M. Joseph, Through the Eyes of John-The Annihilation of Nations, A Walk-Through Heaven, Earth, and Hell is another book that addresses warfare.

Use discernment when making a choice of a book.

Live a normal life, with its "ups and downs," with the limitations of our humanness. If one falters in life or falls unintentionally, pick up your cross and continue on as Christ did. Remember, Christ fell 3 times, so always get up, and keep on fulfilling the Will of God the Father. Live for Our Heavenly Father. Our reward is not of this life but of the next.

Lou, if God be willing, others may write also, in order to help souls.

Until we meet again, John.

O Mary conceived without sin, pray for us who have recourse to you.

PEACE BE UNTO YOU.

BIBLIOGRAPHY

1. Majority of all Christian <u>Bibles</u>
2. <u>The Little Red Book</u>, Hazelden Educational Materials, Center City, Minnesota, 5512-0176, pages 39, 62, 63.
3. Kavanaugh, Kieran, and Rodiguez, Otilio. <u>The Collected Works of St. Teresa of Avila, Vol. two</u>, Washington, D.C.: ICS Publications, Institute of Carmelite Studies, 1980, p. 406.
4. Ibid, pp. 416-417.
5. Kavanaugh, Kieran, and Rodiguez, Otilio. <u>The Collected Works of St. John Of the Cross</u>, Washinton D.C.: ICS Publications, Institute of Carmelite Studies, 1979, p. 384.
6. Kavanaugh, Kieran, and Rodiguez, Otilio. <u>The Collected Works of St. Teresa of Avila, Vol. one.</u> Washington, D.C.: ICS Publications, Institute of Carmelite Studies, 1976, p. 213.
7. Abbey Press Pamphlet #11089, "<u>Our Lady of Fatima's Peace Plan from Heaven</u>," 15 January, 1950: pp.6-7, 12.
8. Kavanaugh, Kieran, and Rodiguez, Otilio. <u>The Collected Works of</u> <u>St. John Of the Cross</u>, Washington, D.C.: ICS Publications, Institute of Carmelite Studies, 1979, p. 385.
9. Kavanaugh, Kieran, and Rodiguez, Otilio. <u>The Collected Works of St. Teresa of Avila, Vol. one</u>, Washington D.C.: ICS Publications, Institute of Carmelite Studies, 1976, p. 204.
10. Ing, Richard. <u>Spiritual Warfare</u>, Whitaker House, 1996. And Blai, Adam C. Hauntings, Possessions, And Exorcisms, 2017.

This is a work of non-fiction. Names, characters, places, and incidences are somewhat altered for privacy and confidential purposes.

www.ingramcontent.com/pod-product-compliance
Lightning Source LLC
LaVergne TN
LVHW091550060526
838200LV00036B/775